Journeys Home

Revealing a Zuni–Appalachia Collaboration

Edited by
Dudley Cocke, Donna Porterfield,
and Edward Wemytewa

Zuni A:shiwi Publishing

Cover illustration: Edward Wemytewa

Interior illustrations: Angelyn DeBord and
　　Edward Wemytewa

Book design: Jane Hillhouse

Photography: Tim Cox

©2002 Idiwanan An Chawe – *Corn Mountain/Pine
　Mountain* script, Zuni stories and songs

©2002 Roadside Theater – *Corn Mountain/Pine
　Mountain* script, Appalachian stories and songs

©2002 Zuni A:shiwi Publishing – *Journeys Home*
　general text

Published by Zuni A:shiwi Publishing
P.O. Box 1009, Zuni, New Mexico 87327

Library of Congress Control Number:
2001 134029

ISBN: 0-9641401-4-4 soft cover

Printed in the U.S.A.

ZUNI
A:SHIWI PUBLISHING

"Difficulty in evaluating, or even discerning,
a particular landscape is related to the distance a culture has
traveled from its own ancestral landscape."

—Barry Lopez, *Arctic Dreams: Imagination and Desire*
in a Northern Landscape (Scribner, NY 1986)

Acknowledgements

It was our good fortune that the staff of Zuni A:shiwi Publishing approached Roadside Theater and Idiwanan An Chawe about making this book after attending a performance of the play *Corn Mountain/Pine Mountain: Following the Seasons.* The idea was enthusiastically supported by the publishing company's board of directors: Georgia Epaloose—president, Malcolm Bowekaty, Jim Enote, Rueben Ghahate, and Tom Kennedy. Anne Beckett, executive director, worked generously with the collaborators to raise funds for the project and conducted interviews with the principals. We are grateful to our production partners, copy editor Liz McGeachy, designer Jane Hillhouse, and illustrator Angelyn DeBord. Further gratitude is extended to Jimmy A'washu for sharing the Turkey Girl story; to Craig McGarvey, who read the draft and provided us with fresh insights; to Elaine and Roger Thomas, who allowed us to turn their Halona B & B into a recording studio; and to Barry Lopez for his encouragement and permission to quote from *Arctic Dreams.* Taki Telonidis and Hal Cannon joined the project to produce the compact disc, and their abiding enthusiasm has ended up informing all of the work.

We wish to thank the National Endowment for the Arts, the Rockefeller Foundation, the Wallace-Reader's Digest Funds, and the Ruth Mott Fund for their financial support of the cultural exchange and artistic collaboration between Roadside Theater/Appalshop and Idiwanan An Chawe/Zuni Rainbow Project. The Rainbow Project was administered by the Pueblo of Zuni, Hayes Lewis, tribal administrator. For their support of this book, we thank the William and Flora Hewlett Foundation, the Andrew W. Mellon Foundation, the Witter Bynner Foundation, the Doris Duke Charitable Foundation, the LEF Foundation, the Appalshop Production and Education Fund, the Indian Set-Aside Funds, the First Nations Development Institute, Theatre Communications Group, and the Santa Fe Art Institute. Foundations take chances on unusual projects because of unusual individuals working within them. Without Melanie Beene (Hewlett), Catherine Wichterman (Mellon), Holly Sidford (Reader's Digest Funds), Sonja Kravanja and Stephen Schwartz (Witter Bynner), Olga Garay (Duke), and Marina Drummer (LEF) there would be no occasion for this acknowledgement.

Finally, we'd like to express our gratitude to all the Zuni and Appalachian families who extended gracious hospitality to us . . . for the healthy food, the good conversation, and the laughter.

Table of Contents

Note: In *Journeys Home*, the word Zuni is used generically, as it is used by the Zuni people, to mean the Zuni Pueblo, one Zuni person, many Zuni people, all Zuni people, and the Zuni language. For example, I am going to Zuni to see a Zuni friend whose family is Zuni, all of whom speak fluent Zuni. In their own language, *Shiwi'ma Bena:we*, such differences are finely delineated.

*Sixteen hundred miles separate
Zuni's Corn Mountain, Dowa Yalanne,
from Appalachia's Pine Mountain.*

Revealing a Zuni–Appalachia Collaboration

Foreword

by Gregory Cajete

The stories of *Journeys Home* are stories of origin: about how things came to be, about why things are the way they are, and about the relationships of humans with plants, animals, and mountains. They are stories of childhood memories and of similar experiences with life's hardships. They are stories and songs of respect: respect for corn and for planting; respect for Turkey Spirits whose sharing of their life ensures the continuance of human life. They are stories of the difficulty of keeping traditions going in the face of rapid social and technological change, where the vicarious experience provided by the TV, the DVD, and the Internet has usurped the direct experience. They are stories of the spirits, good and bad, that inhabit our communal world.

In many ways, Zuni Pueblo, New Mexico, one of the oldest continually occupied settlements in North America, is as different from the settlements in Appalachia's eastern Kentucky as can be imagined. But there are easily overlooked similarities as well. Both places are rural, off the beaten track; they are places that most Americans pass through on their way to someplace else; they are places where people still tell stories directly to one another.

Humans are storytelling animals. Story is a primary linguistic structure through which we think and communicate. We make stories, tell stories, and live stories because it is such an integral part of being human. For example, myths, legends, and folk tales have been a cornerstone of teaching in every culture. These forms of story teach us about human nature in its many dimensions and manifestations. The stories we live by actively shape and integrate our life experience. They inform us, as well as form us.

"In reality, every story is renewed each time and in each place it is told. Stories live through each teller and through each audience which hears and actively engages them."

Foreword, conclusion

There are as many ways to tell a story as there are storytellers, and as many ways to hear a story as well. American Indian tribes created a variety of vehicles—spoken word, song, dance, craft, and visual art—to access the inherent energy and knowledge contained in their body of stories. While keeping true to the core meanings of their stories, tribal storytellers continually improvised, reorganized, and recreated the particular elements of a story to fit their audience, the time and place, and their own personal expression. In reality, every story is renewed each time *and* in each place it is told. Stories live through each teller and through each audience which hears and actively engages them. Stories and their enactment in every form was the way a tribe remembered its shared experience as a People.

The stories in *Journeys Home* are remembered in the heart. They emphasize the importance of maintaining a way of language . . . a loving way of speaking about life and experiences. Feeling the rhythm of the storytellers' language is to feel the rhythm of their Peoples' spirit and of the remembered earth of their communities.

I invite you to journey to Appalachia's Pine Mountain . . . to journey to Zuni's Corn Mountain . . . and to find some of your own journey in the stories of these *Journeys Home*.

May the Good Spirits guide you.

Gregory Cajete
Santa Clara Pueblo, New Mexico

Introduction

by the editors

Journeys Home is the story of the sixteen-year collaboration between artists from two cultures. Sixteen hundred miles west to east across the United States separate Zuni's Corn Mountain from Appalachia's Pine Mountain, while nine thousand years of history in North America separate the Native American experience from the European American experience. How then did traditional artists from these two distinct cultures come to make plays together? This is the story of Journeys Home.

Whitesburg, Kentucky When we started Roadside Theater back in 1975, we asked ourselves, *What would it be like for rural Appalachia to have a professional theater company and a body of original Appalachian drama?* We joined up with some other young people who had grown up in the coalfields of Appalachia. They had started a media arts organization in Whitesburg, Kentucky, called the Appalachian Film Workshop, soon to be known as Appalshop.

Founded in 1969 as part of a national War on Poverty job training program for disadvantaged youth, Appalshop unexpectedly turned its attention to telling the Appalachian story to the region and nation from the inside-out. Its medium was documentary film, and its subjects were local people and events—a hog butchering, the birth of twins assisted by a midwife, foot washing at the Old Regular Baptist Church.

Filmmaking led these young people to an astounding discovery: their Appalachian pictures and the stories that they told had more substance and truth than those made in Los Angeles or New York City. This was an empowering realization for those of us who had too often seen ourselves portrayed by the mass media as hillbillies—inferior folk from corrupted bloodlines.

"Roadside's audience was coalminers and farmers, preachers and teachers, the employed and the unemployed, and everyone's extended family."

Appalshop youth were suddenly turning the stereotype on its head, and word was spreading across the rural region.

Just as there had been no Appalachian filmmaking tradition prior to 1969, in 1975 there was no regional habit of attending or making theater. Excited by Appalshop's idea of telling the Appalachian story in the Appalachian voice, a half-dozen youth asked themselves, *Theater-wise, what does our Appalachian culture have going for it?* The ready answer was the traditions we'd all grown up with—storytelling, balladry, oral histories, and dramatic church services, all living and breathing in a rich regional dialect. These local traditions became the foundation for Roadside Theater's twenty-six-year experiment with drama.

Since we had little money, a scattered population, and no building with a theater, we began as a touring company, often performing in a revival-style tent pitched in church yards, next to community centers and schools, up the hollows of our mountains. Roadside's audience was coalminers and farmers, preachers and teachers, the employed and the unemployed, and everyone's extended family. The lives and stories of these people became the source material for our plays, our performances a way to thank our people for their gift.

As the attraction of Roadside Theater's plays and our way of playmaking spread beyond Appalachia, we began collaborating with other artists and communities wanting to tell their stories from the inside-out. That's when we began visiting Zuni Pueblo in New Mexico, at first performing in the schools and eventually with traditional Zuni artists.

"In the 1960s there were still many Zuni
storytellers to be heard, but by the late 1970s, the radio
and television had become our storytellers and our own traditional
storytellers were no longer invited into our homes."

Zuni, New Mexico It was through our sixteen-year cultural exchange with Roadside Theater and Appalachia that Idiwanan An Chawe emerged here in Zuni. It was a slow birth, beginning with just watching Roadside do its thing in our schools. Their storytelling and singing style was like nothing any of us had ever seen, and our youth really responded to it. Gradually, following the lead of the young people, several of us working in the middle school began sharing some of our traditional culture with the Roadside performers—our songs, dances, and stories. And we began taking some of our students to visit Roadside in their mountain home. That was an eye-opener, because most of us had never been out of the Southwest, much less to Appalachia.

The experience of these visits led us to the idea of finding a way to support our Zuni storytelling tradition. In the 1960s there were still many Zuni storytellers to be heard, but by the late 1970s, the radio and television had become our storytellers and our own traditional storytellers were no longer invited into our homes. So we invited one of our traditional storytellers into the middle school. Her session with the students was not successful. We realized that our young people had never learned the Zuni storytelling etiquette—they didn't understand their role as listener and encourager. After we explained the etiquette to them, they invited a story-teller to a dinner they cooked. The lesson paid off. The kids were very respectful, so the storyteller, feeling comfortable, sat down after dinner and told stories. Captured by the stories, the students had many questions for us at school the next day. Eventually, some of us younger adults began learning the old stories and telling them together at the middle school.

In 1995, we began collaborating with Roadside on an original, bilingual play, *Corn Mountain/Pine Mountain: Following the Seasons.* Well, if you're going to start creating plays, it follows that you need a theater company, and that's how Idiwanan An Chawe was born. *Corn Mountain/Pine Mountain* premiered in Zuni on February 16, 1996, and in Whitesburg on March 15, 1996. Since then we have toured the play to some very interesting places, like New Orleans.

Idiwanan An Chawe means Children of the Middle Place, and is another name for the Zuni people. We continue to tell stories in our Zuni schools, and we now also make original plays drawn from our culture's song, dance, costuming, oral history, and storytelling traditions. Tribally sponsored, we rely on the knowledge of community elders and are especially concerned with providing opportunities for our young people to participate.

All of Idiwanan An Chawe's plays are about our place, and often they confront issues swirling around the health and care of our reservation. For example, *Ma'l Okyattsik An Denihalowilli:we (Gifts from Salt Woman)* is a play about the physical and spiritual care of the Zuni Salt Lake. The play raises issues of United States government violation of Zuni sovereignty rights. Our plays (and radio dramas, which we also produce) are written and performed in the Zuni language, *Shiwi'ma Bena:we.*

When Roadside Theater and Zuni began working together, we were young. With the light-heartedness of youth, we committed ourselves to a twenty-year collaboration. Now sixteen years older, we agree that twenty is too short.

The Zuni Language Shiwi'ma Bena:we

by Wilfred Eriacho, Sr. and Edward Wemytewa

The story of the Zuni language is a story about tradition, religion, education, and interference. The very name Zuni was coined by Spanish chroniclers in 1539. We call ourselves *A:shiwi*. One Zuni person is *Shiwi*. The language of the *A:shiwi* is *Shiwi'ma Bena:we*. Unlike most languages, such as English with its Germanic roots, *Shiwi'ma Bena:we* is a language isolate, which means that it is unrelated to any known language, even to those languages of our pueblo neighbors to the east along the Rio Grande and our Hopi neighbors to the west. *Shiwi'ma Bena:we* is a living language and is spoken by all *A:shiwi* people today. The amount of Zuni spoken and its overall quality varies, of course, and both have been affected by the separation of generations caused by new settlement patterns, by the introduction of other languages, notably English, and in the last fifty years by the electronic media's version of English, such as we hear on television.

Traditionally, the *A:shiwi* lived in close quarters in a pueblo composed of a plaza surrounded by apartment-style adobe buildings, sometimes rising eight stories. People of all ages lived together. Today, although changed in appearance, the old pueblo is still where most of the communal houses, the kivas, and the religious dance halls are located. In the center of the pueblo is a shrine that designates the Heart. The village's physical environ-ment has been as essential to the transmission of our traditions as the presence of our grandmothers and grandfathers. Over the past thirty years, partly in response to our growing population (now numbering 10,000) and to federal government housing regulations, many Zunis have moved away from the Heart into single-family houses, each, seemingly, with its own satellite dish. These solo houses are spread out over several wide areas of the reservation. How, then, in these modern circumstances, will *Shiwi'ma Bena:we* be perpetuated?

voices

Paul Neha, *cultural mentor*

"*Some old language that some people used to use, my grandma used to use, it's no longer here. The reason the younger people are having a hard time understanding the prayer language is because it's entirely different from the everyday language we use here; it's old time language.*

Then, too, awhile back we encouraged our people to pick up the English language, because with English language you can get a job anyplace—go off the reservation, get a job. You can know everything about Zuni language, but you can't get a job on the outside because nobody will understand you."

An Oral Tradition Accommodates the Written

Nurtured by a highly developed oral tradition containing a thousand years of knowledge, stories, beliefs, and histories, we Zuni did not find it necessary to invent our alphabet until thirty years ago. In order to create a written *Shiwi'ma Bena:we*, a certain amount of standardization was required.

Our alphabet is phonetic, adopted from the English alphabet. However, there are eight English characters not included in the Zuni alphabet. They are: f, g, j, q, r, v, x, and z. New characters have been added as well: **ch', ' , : , k', ł, ts'**. Two letters, p and t, can be found in the middle of a word but can never initiate a word. A glottal stop (') coupled with a **ch**, **k**, or **ts** is sometimes referred to as "popped," as sound is forced by air built up at the back of the mouth. A glottal stop (') after a vowel shortens the duration of sound. A colon (:) is only used after a vowel and doubles the vowel's sound in length. A glottal stop after a consonant, usually at the end of a syllable, abruptly stops the sound. The slash (**ł**) sound is sometimes written **łth**, and the sound is produced by saying the **l** and **th** simultaneously. The tongue is pressed against the soft palate and air is directed on either side of it.

The structure of *Shiwi'ma Bena:we* easily accommodates the invention of new words to describe new phenomena. By

Zuni Word	Pronunciation	Word Construction	English Translation
benałashshi:we	bay-nah-lthäsh-she-way	bena:we (language, story) + łashshi:we (ancient)	ancient tales, historical accounts
ho'habonna	hoe-hä-bone-näh	ho'i (alive, people) + habonna (will gather)	audience or gathering
sonahchi	sown-ah-chee	son (we were [hons]) + ahchi (right? [hatchi?])	once upon a time (beginning of a fable or fictitious story; storyteller says, "We were. Right?" Audience answers, "Right!")

combining or accenting root words in different ways and by adding prefixes and suffixes, a single new word can be made from many words, and this new word can be understood by any Zuni. This word construction also helps Zuni scholars understand ancient words such as the names of places and classifications of the natural world.

Ancient History

Traditional stories tell us that our ancient *A:shiwi* ancestors, the *Ino:de:kwe*, originated at the Grand Canyon and then migrated south and east, searching for the Middle Place, where they finally settled some 900 years ago in present day eastern Arizona and western New Mexico. While there must have been multilingual and multicultural environments in ancient *A:shiwi* communities, *Shiwi'ma Bena:we* was always the dominant language of the *A:shiwi*. Through and with it, every component of the world was interpreted, understood, and conveyed. Through and with it, non-Zuni knowledge and activities were assimilated into the total context of *A:shiwi* culture.

The *A:shiwi* concept of spirituality, of self, of life, of survival was synonymous with place. Working in harmony with their semi-arid desert home, our *A:shiwi* ancestors developed successful agricultural methods based on a complex knowledge of their ecology. They constructed metaphorical language to communi-

Zuni Word	Pronunciation	Word Construction	English Translation
le:' semkoni'kya	lay-sam-caw-nee-kyä	le:wi' (this much) + sem (fable, half true story) + koni'kya (was short)	end of story (This is how short the story was. [for a tale of any length])
odin łana	oh-din-lthä-näh	odinne (act of dancing) + łana (big in size, number)	climax in a dance or many groups of dancers
iho'iya:k'yanna	ee-hoe-ee-yäh-kgyän-näh	iho (become person) + iya:k'yanna (become mature)	become a mature person

cate this knowledge. For example, the word _Nana:kwe_ translated literally means grandfathers. The _Nana:kwe_ are the spirits of our early ancestors, who take the form of water to bless the crops and the parched land. Stories about the _Nana:kwe_ taught the ancestors about rain—how to respect it, how to attract it, and how to make the most of it when it came.

Traditionally, Zuni language education occurred in the context of daily life. Children learned formally and informally by observing, listening, imitating, visualizing, memorizing, participating, repeating, and practicing. All knowledge and skills had immediate useful application and purpose. In most learning situations, people of all ages were involved, so children learned from several adults in one setting.

Recent History

In 1539-40, the _A:shiwi_ first encountered Europeans in the persons of Father Marcos de Niza, his scout Estevan (an African slave), and Coronado and his Spanish army. Coronado was looking to strike it rich by looting the fabled Seven Cities of Gold, which Father Marcos reported that he had discovered. Coronado and his army arrived in Zuni expecting to be blinded by the glitter of gold; instead, they found seven pueblos constructed of stone and plastered with mud, the Seven Cities of _Cibola_. Deflated, they decided to claim all _A:shiwi_ people and their land for Spain. For some unknown reason, the Spaniards began calling us Zuni. We named them in our language _tsibolo:wa_ or _Tsibolo:wa:kwe_. This translates in English to _tsiwe_/body hair, _bololo:we_/bundle or roll of and _kwe_/people.

The Spaniards immediately began forcing the Catholic religion and education on the people, young and old, but this persecution was met with steadfast resistance. For example, in 1680 the _A:shiwi_ and their neighboring Pueblo tribes staged a coordinated revolt in the Southwest, sending those Spaniards who were not killed packing for El Paso del Norte. The _A:shiwi_ then moved atop _Dowa Yalanne_, Corn Mountain, and from this stronghold kept the Spanish army at bay for eleven years, until an uneasy peace was proclaimed.

After two hundred and eighty-two years of rule, the Spanish ceded Zuni to Mexico, and from 1821 to 1846, the Mexican government held political jurisdiction over our lands. During this brief period, there was minimal interference from Mexican bureaucrats, military, and priests, and the traditional ways of Zuni religion and education continued.

1846 to the present marks the period of United States

government influence and interference. For thirty years, from 1846 to 1876, the American government's Indian Bureau delegated responsibility to and financially supported two Protestant religious groups to educate and Americanize the Zuni. Their assignment was to eradicate as much of the Zuni heritage as possible and to replace it with their European-derived culture and Christianity. Children were severely punished for speaking *Shiwi'ma Bena:we* at school. Protestant church officials and staff not only concerned themselves with the children's education but also interfered with traditional religious activities. On several occasions, they called out the Tenth Calvary from Fort Wingate, New Mexico, in an attempt to stop traditional dances and other religious practices. By 1850, European-derived disease, diet, and alcohol had killed 90 percent of the Zuni people, leaving only about a thousand *A:shiwi* in the world.

From 1876 until 1956, the United States Bureau of Indian Affairs officially took over the responsibility for assimilating the Zuni, and of course the language of instruction continued to be solely English. But English was not the only European language we *A:shiwi* heard, especially during the 1800s, as many different European peoples came to Zuni for one reason or another. We called these visitors *Lulu* or *Lulu:kwe* because their speech sounded like the lululululululu, the sound of the housefly.

From 1956 to 1980, responsibility for educating Zuni children was passed to the state of New Mexico. In the beginning, the state continued the practices of the Bureau of Indian Affairs. However, from 1968 to 1973, the state legislature passed laws to fund, develop, and implement bilingual education, and the federal government legislated discretionary programs and allocated funds to address the educational needs of minority language students. As a result, the Zuni culture gained some acceptability in the school environment. The gain was short-lived, however, as bilingual programs were curtailed when federal funding ended.

After much debate in the Zuni community and a referendum, the Zuni School District was created on July 1, 1980. Although we finally gained control of our public schools, many problems remain to be solved. Bilingual programs struggle to find footholds and have not been fully implemented at all grade levels. While some teachers accept bilingual education, few are trained in it, and bilingual educational materials are scarce.

Perpetuation

The *Shiwi Messenger*, our community newspaper, periodically features articles written in *Shiwi'ma Bena:we*, and the A:shiwi A:wan Museum and Heritage Center creates language exhibits. Over time, the community has recorded many elderly people to establish a resource of old spoken *Shiwi'ma Bena:we*. Idiwanan An Chawe performs Zuni language plays on stage and radio. The Natural Resource Department and a number of related, culturally based conservation programs preserve some of the names of places and the agricultural and ecological language of our ancestors.

Religious efforts to perpetuate our language take place, as they always have, in the kivas and medicine societies and through the Rain Priesthood. Throughout the year, as part of a calendar of religious activities, such as night dances, rain dances, and *Sha'lako*, ancient prayers, epic poems, and chants are recited by young and old. The full embodiment of the Zuni language is present in these rituals; the words are sacred because they convey the cultural memory, the breath of the ancient ones.

It is this language that encapsulates the spirit of the people, connecting us to the knowledge that centers us, both individually and communally. It is this language that makes us *A:shiwi*.

voices

Edward Wemytewa

"In the 1960s, many of the stories of our elders were collected. I remember one storyteller had filled twenty-five reel-to-reel tapes with stories. When we were creating the alphabet in the '70s, I went back to these stories. We also invited elderly people from the community to come and sit and help us clarify words and concepts. In the process, something unexpected happened—I started feeling more in touch with my soul and my spirit. It was not only because I was again writing and thinking in Zuni, it was because I was relating to our forefathers' philosophy—to what they felt, what they valued. And I was having to look at myself, because I talked about values, but didn't really follow the values. It felt like I was waking up after a long sleep."

Appalachia Historical Background

by the editors

The Appalachian Mountain region stretches from Maine to Georgia. It is an economically and culturally diverse territory with twenty-two million people. Roadside Theater's home is in central Appalachia, where the 110-mile long Pine Mountain forms the spine of the densely forested Cumberland Plateau. Located in present day southwest Virginia, upper east Tennessee, eastern Kentucky, and southern West Virginia, where the four states back up on one another, the Cumberland Plateau was once hunting ground for the Cherokee and other Native tribes. The first Europeans to arrive on the Plateau were Scotch-Irish. They came to the frontier as much to escape their Old World nemesis, the English (who had already captured the continent's eastern seaboard), as to satisfy their adventuresome spirits.

From the beginning of the Scotch-Irish settlement on the Cumberland Plateau, there was intermarriage with Native Americans. In October, 1838, the Cherokee were rounded up by the United States Army for their final forced march west, "The Trail of Tears." Some of those Cherokee sought to escape death by hiding in the mountains. Today, the majority of Appalachian families settling prior to 1900 on the Cumberland Plateau have Indian blood in their veins.

It was not until the 1890s that railroads and capitalism reached the Cumberlands. Businessmen from the east (and a few from Europe) came seeking their fortunes in the rich coal and timber fields in one of the oldest standing mountain ranges in the world. Some locals quickly bought into the outsiders' program of progress with its new law and order, banks, and written contracts. Others saw the coming development as leading to the destruction of paradise and the end of a natural way of life. Now a hundred years later, corporations, including transnational corporations, are the absentee owners of 75 percent of central Appalachia's land, its minerals, and its timber. Feeling little obligation to the region's people, these absentee landlords have played a significant role in creating record levels of poverty on the Cumberland Plateau. To spite this economic hardship, mountain people continue to record their own

"The majority of mountain people are unprincipled ruffians. There are two remedies only: education or extermination. The mountaineer, like the red Indian, must learn this lesson."

—*New York Times* editorial, 1912

version of history in an Appalachian oral tradition loaded with cultural memory.

The Great Smoky Mountains of western North Carolina mark an eastern boundary of Appalachia. Tony Earley, author of the next essay, was born and reared in the foothills of the Smokies where wages from factory work mirrored a coalminer's payday on the Cumberland Plateau, and where hillside farmers could count on a few more acres to till than their counterparts to the west. The two places have been and remain at once different and similar in the Appalachian experience that they share.

The Appalachian Dialect

Guilt and the Past Participle:
True Confessions
from the Appalachian Diaspora

by Tony Earley

Although my wife, Sarah, and I grew up outside the same small town in western North Carolina and attended the same public schools, the differences in our backgrounds make our marriage a surprisingly cross-cultural institution. Simply put, Sarah's grandfather owned a textile mill; mine owned a mule. That we grew up in largely different worlds was never more obvious than during our wedding, which we decided—for reasons that grow progressively more mystifying to us in retrospect—should be a full-blown, high church Episcopalian affair. Most of the guests on Sarah's side of the church were lifelong Anglicans, while a high percentage on my side were country Baptists. The scene during communion couldn't have been more chaotic if someone had yelled fire. I watched from the front of the church as my family and friends searched wild-eyed through the *Book of Common Prayer* for a clue as to what they were supposed to do. A longtime friend of mine wound up taking communion twice simply because she had no idea how to escape from the altar rail.

Although the years I spent in college and graduate school, as well as the upwardly mobile pretensions I acquired along the way, have erased most of the superficial social differences between Sarah and me, the subject of class comes up surprisingly often in our day-to-day lives, most often regarding the manner in which I speak when I'm not paying particular attention to the manner in which I speak. Like a lot of people of rural Appalachian descent, I tend to use the past-tense forms of irregular verbs in places where the past-participle form is called for by grammar books. For example, I'm more likely to say, "I could have wrote more," than "I could have written more," which happens to be correct. Class distinction, socio-economic disparity, and the cultural history of the Appalachian region become conversational topics whenever Sarah corrects me. I say, "I should have threw that away." Sarah says, "Thrown." I say, "Don't tell me how to talk." In our household, the sentence "I'm going to lay down and take me a nap" is as likely to lead to an impassioned recitation of how my grandfather had to turn to moonshining to feed his family during the Great Depression as it is to my ever getting to sleep.

The Appalachian Dialect, *continued*

What Sarah has made me aware of is that the tricky part about speaking in the Appalachian vernacular is that while it is at once a socio-cultural signifier that marks its speaker as one who shares in the indigenous history of a particular place, much of it also happens to be grammatically incorrect according to standard English usage. "Correct" and "incorrect" are, of course, artificial constructions and, like all rules, reflect either the will of a dominant power structure or the immense, grinding, more-or-less democratic weight of cultural consensus. That specific regional dialects have been, and will continue to be, marginalized by this process troubles me less than the fact that the Appalachian dialect has been somehow singled out by the greater culture that contains it as the official language of stupidity and ignorance. Indeed, the words "hillbilly" or "redneck" have become the last pejoratives denoting cultural or ethnic stereotypes that Americans can toss about without fear of being slapped with censure by an increasingly politically sensitive culture. As a reasonably well-educated professor of English I can say with almost certain surety that my occasional tendency to choose past-tense forms of irregular verbs when past-participle forms are called for, that my propensity for using "lay" when "lie" is appropriate, that my reflexive conversational fondness for the double negative, are symptomatic of neither ignorance nor stupidity, but rather emblematic of my membership in the cultural heritage of the Appalachians. Still, because I theoretically know better, I can't help but wonder if my choosing to use grammatically incorrect Appalachianisms on purpose would be as artificial as a self-conscious decision to use only proper English when speaking to people who share my social and regional background. All I can say for sure is that talking was a lot easier in the days before I understood the socio-cultural implications of the vernacular in which I naturally speak.

I visited Zuni Pueblo for the first, and so far only time, last December (2000), when Sarah and I spent a week driving around New Mexico. Although everyone we spoke to during our short time at Zuni was cordial to us, I don't think I've ever been more conscious of my whiteness—or uncomfortable

"I'm one of those people who started out poor,
hated being poor, hated being looked down on by people
who weren't, strove consciously to escape . . . succeeded,
then managed to make myself feel guilty about my success."

because of it. I couldn't get beyond the fact that we were white people who had traveled out of our way, at some expense, to basically gawk at people with skins darker than our own. Looking back, it seems to me that my discomfort resulted from two different types of guilt, neither of them particularly noble. The first was simply garden-variety, upper-middle class, liberal white guilt, which I used, in the standard manner, to flagellate myself just enough to make me feel better about my good fortune, but not so much that I would consider renouncing it. The second was a somewhat more complex variety, although that complexity does little to palliate either the guiltiness itself, or my inability to get over it or live with it constructively. I'm one of those people who started out poor, hated being poor, hated being looked down on by people who weren't, strove consciously from early childhood on to escape both poverty and the anonymity that accompanies it, succeeded, then managed to make myself feel guilty about my success. In my case, as it often does, succeeding meant leaving—spiritually, intellectually, geographically. I joined the Episcopal church, the traditional faith of the southern upper class; I at least attempted to cull from my speech the old words and grammatical tics that gave away my rural Appalachian background; I left the part of North Carolina in which my family has lived for two hundred years, and which still is, ironically, the part of the world I love best. Do I wish that I had stayed home, stayed poor, and stayed anonymous? Of course not. Despite these manufactured existential crises, I like it out here. Yet, as with all departures, my leaving forged in me a series of regrets—most of them irrational—at abandoning the things I left behind. Whenever this particular species of guilt is strongest, I often notice—as I did that day in Zuni while ordering lunch—that my Appalachian accent grows noticeably more pronounced, that I seem to be offering ethnicity as a type of apology. It's as if my subconscious is shouting out to anyone who will listen, "Please don't hate me. I haven't always been like this."

In the Zuni museum, Sarah and I spent some time at a display of authentic Zuni handcrafts alongside fake Zuni handcrafts made in the Philippines. We couldn't locate a key identifying which was which,

The Appalachian Dialect, conclusion

and Sarah and I, with our untrained eyes, often couldn't tell the difference. I feel that same kind of confusion when I think about the tenuous place Appalachian vernacular occupies inside the constantly evolving babble of standard American English. Even as I listen to it come out of my own mouth, it's increasingly hard for me to separate the authentic from the ersatz, the sincere from the ironic, the dancer from the dance. That's why—although as a general rule, I hate being corrected about anything—I'm always secretly pleased when I say, "I wish I'd've knew that sooner," and Sarah says, "Known." Because I don't think about it first, I know it's the real deal, that it's Appalachian and that it's old, and that, even as I strive to figure out how to live in this prefabricated future I've constructed for myself, I'm still linked through language, through the breath of speech, to what the novelist Willa Cather (a Virginian who wound up in New York by way of Nebraska and Pittsburgh) called in *My Antonia*, "the precious, the incommunicable past."

The Story of a Collaboration

by Dinah Zeiger

1969 Dudley Cocke and Edward Wemytewa meet on a basketball court.

1984 Roadside Theater informally visits Zuni Pueblo on the tail end of a tour of Utah. (Tommy Bledsoe and Ron Short are mistaken for members of Z Z Top.)

Edward Wemytewa

The collaboration between Roadside and Idiwanan An Chawe is a funny thing because it really started so long ago—thirty or so years ago, when Dudley first visited Zuni, and then Roadside started coming occasionally for performances. Back then I was working with the Zuni Language Curriculum project. We had just invented the Zuni alphabet and wanted to incorporate written Zuni into our public schools, but we didn't have any Zuni language materials to use for that purpose. In 1981, I left to go off to college, and the Language Curriculum project remained dormant until about 1989, when I knew we had to do something about it. We had to make a giant step, and that's when I saw Roadside Theater performing their stories in the classroom and on stage. I saw how they used their traditions in a new way, and I thought—we have to do something like that, something of that caliber, to make the community know that there were still efforts being made to preserve our spoken language and develop the written language.

Dudley Cocke

I first visited Zuni in 1969. I enjoyed the culture and community and the natural beauty, but I also saw the struggle of the Zuni people. It's a lot like Appalachia. We've got a lot of the same troubles and a lot of the same joys, and that's what drew us together. In sharing our troubles and joys we got connected to one another. You could say we're both privileged, because we each have a sense of our history, of heritage, of being part of a special culture. We each have this historical sense of who we are based on our oral traditions.

The Story of a Collaboration, continued

1985 Roadside Theater performs in Zuni elementary and middle schools on the tail end of another western tour.

1986 Roadside Theater members climb *Dowa Yalanne* (Corn Mountain) with Edward Wemytewa and a group of middle school students.

Edward Wemytewa

Roadside had been visiting us for about a decade before we formalized a "Zuni theater troupe." Roadside was doing a residency at the middle school, and I saw that their form of storytelling was similar to our traditional Zuni storytelling. But we had no resources, no pool of storytellers, so I started looking for ways to create a resource pool, and I started talking with Roadside about a collaboration. It was 1995, and Roadside got funds from the Rockefeller Foundation, and we decided to go ahead. I set up a public meeting in Zuni to talk about the collaboration and about fifteen people attended. Well, we invited them back for a second meeting, and nobody showed up! That's when Arden and I knew that if we were going to make this happen, we'd have to do it ourselves. But to tell the truth, we didn't even know what collaboration meant.

Arden Kucate

At first, we didn't think it was going to fly. We were worried that the Zuni audience was used to the traditional form of storytelling and wouldn't like seeing it in a more contemporary setting. We wanted to make the performance livelier, but we didn't want to make it theatrical, with props and backdrops, so we retained the core of the traditional style, but we modified it.

1986–
1989 Roadside Theater visits Zuni several times performing in the schools. By '89, most Zuni youth have seen Roadside perform.

1990 With support from a National Endowment for the Arts grant, Roadside conducts a two-week residency in Zuni, living with Zuni families, performing in the schools, and sharing the stage with Zuni storytellers, singers, and dancers. The residency coincides with Sha'lako, the big year-end religious celebration. (Donna thinks she learns how to make tamales.)

Edward Wemytewa

When no one showed up for that second meeting, Roadside didn't let it drop. They said, "We're going to go on with this plan to make a play together, and you guys will perform it with us on stage. We'll have a formal script." All I could think was, what kind of theater are you talking about?! Zunis don't have theater. Then it dawned on me that we have all kinds of theater. I look in my backyard and we have the rain dances—we have the night dances. It's a different kind of theater, but it's a very rich theater. And then I started thinking about stories and storytelling. I grew up listening to stories and I admire storytellers—some of the materials I wrote for the Zuni Language Curriculum project came out of listening to storytellers. That's when it came to me that our theater project with Roadside—our script—would be an extension of the traditional Zuni storyteller.

Donna Porterfield

One reason this collaboration worked was because of the amount of time over the years we'd spent sharing and learning about each other, not just with Edward but with a lot of other people in Zuni. We got to the point that we could laugh with and at each other—that made the process comfortable. I can't understand all of Zuni culture, but there are some things that have to do with the heart and with feeling that I do understand. Another reason it worked was that the theme of the play—farming—was something we shared. The four of us who were responsible for writing the play are about the same age, and we had grown up in a time when farming was still an important part of life—a really important part of our background.

1991 Roadside Theater member Ron Short visits Zuni on his Harley. (He gets a big discount on jewelry at the Zuni Co-op.)

Edward Wemytewa

In our initial scripting meeting with Roadside we talked about differences and commonalities. How do we deal with differences? Does everything in the script have to be Native? What about language—English or Zuni? We were two diverse groups who knew enough about each other to know we wanted to work together, but no more. Over ten years we'd established some sort of familiarity, but we didn't have a clue about how to proceed. It's like you visit the library, and the librarian stacks a pile of books on the table and you need time to go through them before you know what you learned. At first, I didn't know where to start, what to ask.

We started with a story circle in Kentucky. There are certain rules to a story circle—it has an agreed upon theme or topic that everyone sitting in the circle can choose either to speak about when it's their turn or to pass, if they don't have anything to contribute. It keeps going around that way until no one has anything more to say. It's really a listening circle as much as it is a telling circle.

Arden Kucate

All I knew about Appalachia before this work was that's where hillbillies came from. I'd never met anyone from there. Then we went there, and I visited Tommy Bledsoe way up in the hills. There's another family that lives further up Tommy's hollow, still living a very traditional life. We visited them, and it brought back a lot of good memories about growing up in the same way. But I wasn't living that traditional life any more. These people were still living off the earth and making their own cottage cheese and milking the cow.

1992 Zuni and Appalachian middle school students make and exchange videotapes about their communities. One Zuni video repeatedly talks about going to the sheep camp, but never shows anyone actually arriving at the camp. (Appalachian students appropriate the phrase "going to the sheep camp" to mean skipping school.)

Edward Wemytewa

During the story circles we talked about ourselves, our experiences and what we hoped to get out of the project. In addition to the artists, there were Roadside administrative staff in the story circle, too. We didn't know them, but since they'd be involved in the project it was important for us to know them. We shared some ideas there, and when we came back here, Arden and I started looking for resources, collecting stories, and thinking about singing. Our stories often have refrains that are sung, but music itself isn't part of our storytelling tradition. We knew there was no way that Zuni was going to become Appalachia or the other way around. The whole point was to stay who we were and to use the cultural expressions that we knew.

Arden Kucate

When questions came up about what was appropriate, we worked around it by making sure that everyone—the cast and the core group—sat around the table, looked at the script and talked it out. Everyone was entitled to their own opinion, and that made us comfortable collaborating with another group. All those hours spent sitting around the table and discussing it—voicing our pros and cons—made it easier on stage, because we knew that we were in consensus.

1993 Summer: Edward Wemytewa and Arden Kucate visit Roadside's home in Virginia and Kentucky to plan an exchange. (Arden, who has never seen a lightning bug, has a close encounter with a bunch of them attracted to the phosphorescent paint on his t-shirt.)

Edward Wemytewa

A big decision was whether the Zuni stories would be in Zuni or English. I decided the Zuni stories would all be in Zuni, which meant I had to summarize them for Ron and Donna, so they could begin to write a script that would link the stories together. The Zuni language is complex, and we wanted to make sure our partners and our audiences—both here in Zuni and elsewhere—understood. A lot of our own Zuni kids don't understand the subtleties of their language. We needed a bilingual script—English was necessary for non-Zuni speakers and even for some who speak our language—to make sure everyone could understand the nuances of the Zuni stories. We want our language to continue to live and we want other responsible people in Zuni, in public positions, to use the language and maintain it at a high level.

1993 Winter: Four Zuni adult artists and four Zuni students participate in a residency in Virginia and Kentucky, living with Roadside members, performing in the schools, conducting workshops, and sharing the stage with Roadside artists. (Sixth grade girls at Norton Elementary School fall in love with Joey Zunie; Arden is mistaken for a tall Mexican, which becomes his new nickname.)

Edward Wemytewa

Arden and I were trying to figure out what would interest our audience, which meant we had to think about who we were telling the stories to. I came up with this idea about farming because it's an essential part of Zuni culture. It was the strength of the people who endured on this arid land. Why is corn so important? Why do we have rain dances? Farming stories helped me classify the Kachinas, the seeds. These stories helped me break down our social and religious structure and comprehend who we are.

Arden started sharing with me stories that had religious and philosophical connotations for Zuni. It was exciting to re-acquaint ourselves with storytelling. We familiarized ourselves with as many stories as we could find. One night, sitting with Arden, I started to summarize them, and the play's story just flowed out. I didn't really even know what I said, but in essence it was the spine of *Corn Mountain/Pine Mountain*. Later on we added *Following the Seasons*—winter, spring, summer, and fall. It came from just talking first. Once we had that spine, farming, it made us believe we could actually come up with something coherent.

Arden Kucate

The season theme really started when Roadside came for a visit and Ron Short and I took a ride out in the country to Nutria, where I was raised. We were sitting outside my grandma's old house talking about the seasons. I was telling him about how when we planted corn or other seeds we gave one for Earth, one for the crow, and so on. All the time, Ron was listening and processing, and that conversation in Nutria became part of one of the songs he wrote about following the seasons. It's a song about two worlds, with miles of difference between them, and how the seasons and planting were the same. That song is another story about how Appalachia and Zuni collaborated.

The Story of a Collaboration, continued

1994 The Rockefeller Foundation gives money to support the new play collaboration.

1995 Spring: Dudley Cocke, Ron Short, and Donna Porterfield visit Zuni to work on the play. (All the collaborators get the flu.)

Edward Wemytewa

Putting the pieces together was something else. We didn't even know what a formal script looked like. And then the Roadside folks started using theater terminology, and I said, "Wait a minute, you're going to have to explain that." And I had to push myself to actually write down the stories. We talked to Roadside on the phone a lot. Arden and I decided that we were just going to have to trust the professionals, so we left the script up to them. We sent Roadside what we had, and they put the stories together to create something new.

Arden Kucate

It was when Roadside added their part that the pieces fell into place. It took time to learn that new style, because traditional storytelling has no script and the storyteller just sits in one place. The script helped fit together two groups, put them in the same setting.

1995 Summer: Edward
Wemytewa, Arden
Kucate, and others visit
Roadside to work on the
play. (Everybody eats way
too many "'maters".)

1995 Fall: Stories and songs are
exchanged via mail.

Donna Porterfield

When it came to the writing, we'd mail
our ideas and stories back and forth. One
time Edward sent us some material and in
it was a story about a bear. Ron and I
looked at it, and we just said there isn't
any way this story will fit. I put off calling
Edward to tell him because I thought
maybe he really liked this bear and really
wanted it in the script. Then one day he
called me and said, "You know, Arden
and I have been thinking about that bear
story and we don't think it fits the script."
It just seemed like a lot of times it went
that way, which was a good sign to me,
because I was nervous about doing this in
a way that would make sense and honor
both traditions. So much damage has
been done by outsiders meddling in each
others' cultures, and I knew from experience that things can happen in the heat
of a collaboration.

The Story of a Collaboration, continued

1996 January: *Corn Mountain/Pine Mountain: Following the Seasons* script is assembled.

1996 February: Roadside travels to Zuni to rehearse and premiere *Corn Mountain/ Pine Mountain*. (Roadside learns about Zuni time.)

Edward Wemytewa

Our stories speak of ancient values and how we see ourselves today. The script was organized around a variety of old and modern stories, with songs and dances woven in. The stories and dances in the play are different than our religious recitations and dances, but in the play we use them in much the same way— to give the audience a new experience, a chance to relax and reflect.

When the final script arrived, it was the first time I'd ever really seen one. We'd seen Shakespearean scripts in our school books—seeing something like that could scare anybody. So I was hesitant, but curious, too. I was kind of elated, to be honest, but then I wondered if we could pull it off.

Ron Short

I think music and dance are at the heart of the play. While the stories talk very directly about the two cultures, the songs and dances reveal the subtlety of cultural expression, the deep-felt expressions of self that have been defined and refined through many generations. In both communities that learning process has happened in the same way—singers have taught singers, dancers have taught dancers. Across the generations the identity of the culture has passed internally through the people.

Dudley Cocke

I see a fair amount of professional theater, and if I look at the singing and dancing and costumes in *Corn Mountain/Pine Mountain* in theatrical terms, it's magnificent. It's grander than Broadway. But I think at times it is hard to recognize the richness that is around us until we get a little distance.

1996 March: Idiwanan An Chawe travels to Whitesburg to rehearse and premiere *Corn Mountain/Pine Mountain.* (Idiwanan An Chawe learns about Roadside's stage timing.)

Edward Wemytewa

At first all I wanted to do was write it, then get somebody else up there on stage to perform it. Somebody articulate, with a pleasant voice who can actually sing. Not me; I don't even sing in the shower. My role was to provide the information for the stories. I wanted to make sure that as a tribe, as a person involved in the language, we had a product that the community could use. But as the project went on, no lead person appeared to take it on stage, and that's how I ended up there. I wanted our language to be demonstrated in public. Our traditional storytellers used to do this, but they had disappeared. So, looking at the Roadside model, I thought it was the best alternative. And I wanted it to succeed.

Arden Kucate

It was a challenge because rather than reciting things you knew from within, you had a script to memorize. That was a significant change. It involved hours of trying to learn it, and a lot of times it was frustrating. We had to learn how to synchronize with another group so the stories would flow freely rather than cutting abruptly from one to the other. We had to streamline the transitions. That's when we added the dances to give us a little time to re-group and get ready for the next story. It took time, and we were all new to it, so we had to rely on one another, to coach each other all the way through.

The Story of a Collaboration, continued

1996–2000 *Corn Mountain/Pine Mountain* goes on tour. Cast size varies from eleven to twenty-two according to the number of young dancers.

Edward Wymetewa

We had a week of rehearsals with Roadside before the first performance, to work out transitions and choreography. Dudley was the director, but we'd all get involved in trying to stage it. Then it would get chaotic and he'd take control again because there were too many directors. Finally he and Arden put it together. Arden's been dancing all his life and knows the traditional ways and how things should be done. They worked out what the performance should look like.

Coming from a very close community, one of our big fears was that we might be laughed at, that people would be rude. The first performance, we came out on stage with withdrawn faces. I mean we were nervous. I would be looking at Arden and his foot would be tapping and his hands would be in his pockets, and I said to myself, "He's doing the worst, the things that we are not supposed to do," and after a while, I would be tapping my foot, too. And again, we weren't sure if we were connecting with the audience. But I think one of the things the people in Zuni saw and began to believe was that a Zuni can stand up there and talk fluently in our native language.

Ron Short

I don't think they (Edward, Arden, and Dinanda) recognized that they were the pros when it came to being Zuni storytellers. When they came to Kentucky, people were dazzled by the costumes, the sound of the language. That had never happened before, to them or to us. People in Kentucky came to see Roadside in a different way because we were standing beside the Zuni on that stage.

Ron Short

From the beginning Edward and Arden insisted that young people be involved, that it would not be just older people performing. There had to be a way for young people to participate who didn't have time to learn the script. At first it was a concern but it became one of the better things about the collaboration, being able to have six or sixteen dancers. That's part of Zuni culture.

Dudley Cocke

We were performing once at D. Y. Elementary School and we had maybe eight young dancers in the show. But word got around that it was alright to join, so the next night we had maybe seventeen who wanted to dance. I was backstage, and every time their cue came, the kids would line up, and as they hit the stage, they'd take off their glasses—most Zunis wear glasses. By the time everyone got on stage, I had glasses coming out of every pocket.

Edward Wemytewa

The collaboration and performance made us come out of our shell. We'd traveled and done cultural exchanges before this collaboration, but we still had this "stoic Indian" kind of expression. But we got over it—sometimes by making faces at Dudley. Suddenly we had to be aware of where we were on stage in relation to everyone else; it was all so new. We stumbled many times, but we were, as Ron says, "getting growed."

Now we're at the point where we get stronger when we're up there on stage. Even if your spirit isn't right, you're empowered the more you're up there. And so sometimes if you start speaking and you are self-conscious, you just jump into the story. The story is important, so you just make yourself insignificant and the story significant, and that is what it becomes, and that is what it is about. And so this work has actually helped me hang onto a lot of other things in my life.

Dinanda Laconsello

I saw Roadside perform at the middle school where I work, and I fell in love with their stories. So when Edward approached me to become part of the cast, I decided to take a risk. I really didn't grow up hearing stories. My time and age was with the TV and electricity being here, so I think that was the reason I had a strong belief in becoming a storyteller and just being able to learn.

Donna Porterfield

You know, at Roadside we want audiences who are participants, not just spectators. We want to have a real exchange, and that just can't happen without a lot of audience engagement work, starting on the front end of it all and following it on out. So I think we spent as much time building an audience as developing the play.

Edward Wemytewa

I think the reason why our stories work and why as storytellers we've continued to tell them is because we realized we weren't only creating a story but an audience, too. We were training ourselves and our audiences. It wasn't just going up on the stage but into the classroom, out in the community.

Children Who Made Dragonfly is a story in one of our later plays, and at the end of the performance we passed out cornstalk dragonflies that we made for the children in the audience. But it was the old people— the grandmothers—who said, "I didn't get one, give me one." They reached out for this cornstalk dragonfly, and they inhaled its spirit. We believe that everything we make is a part of us, therefore it is alive. By inhaling the spirit, the grandmas were blessing and welcoming the new life that we had made. Everyone felt this was a very warm ending to the performance, an ending we could not have scripted.

Kim Neal Cole

I didn't really know much about Zuni, and when I got there I realized their stories were like our front porch stories, not separate from everyday life. I would sit in Edward's mother's house and watch Mudheads (*sacred clowns*) pass by outside; that's when you know you are *in* it. You are there, and it is going on all around you.

The Story of a Collaboration, continued

Edward Wemytewa

We learned a lot from working with Roadside, and they learned from us—we found a lot of things we share. And the Zuni community found out how much they are interested in other cultures. You can't predict a product, but when it's finished, it's special because, through the process, you've grown, you've pushed yourself and learned.

Ron Short

Responses from our home audiences have been better than responses elsewhere. Most people not connected to Zuni or Appalachia are faced with two unknown cultures. And people who are used to other kinds of theater often don't know what to make of what's happening—with performers coming on dancing in an extraordinary way and more than one storyline and language. Nothing about it fits the stereotype.

Dudley Cocke

It's true. The performers are not taking on Appalachian and Zuni roles—they are Appalachian and Zuni people. They embody their culture, and this gives the performance a ritualistic cast. This can disorient audiences.

Ron Short

Some audiences decide the play is an intellectual test. Others try to see it as pure song and dance. Either way, they simply don't have enough context to understand it as a gift, which is how our Zuni and Appalachian audiences see it. If theater is a place where we enact who we are, the question becomes: How much do you simplify yourself and your culture in order to entertain people? How much can you give up and still hold onto yourself?

Anne Beckett conducted the extensive interviews upon which this story is based.

Revealing a Zuni–Appalachia Collaboration

A Note About the Play and Its Translation

The place and time of *Corn Mountain/Pine Mountain* is the here and now. The players are six storytellers, who are on the stage at all times, and anywhere from five to sixteen Zuni dancers and singers who enter and exit. Elaborate, traditional Zuni dance regalia is worn in all performances. The scenic and lighting designs vary according to venue: from the simple for a community center to the complex for a large auditorium. Consistent design elements include several roughly hewn wooden benches, Appalachian quilts, Zuni blankets, and different lighting for the play's various performance components—storytelling, singing, oral history narration, and dance.

It may help the reader imagine the play to know that it is performed in a mix of English and Zuni, and that the ratio of English to Zuni varies in a performance depending on the audience. For non-Zuni audiences, the Zuni stories are often told in a combination of Zuni and English. The Appalachian parts are in English regardless of who is in the audience.

Wilfred Eriacho, Sr. and Edward Wemytewa are responsible for the Zuni language. Both were instrumental in the creation of the Zuni alphabet in the 1970s. Half jokingly, they attributed any difference of opinion about spelling or sentence construction to their growing up in the pueblo on opposite sides of the Zuni River. The Zuni River (now a dry ditch) is twenty yards wide.

As for the Zuni to English translation, Dudley Cocke and Edward Wemytewa have tried to capture some of the subtlety of the Zuni language without resulting in stilted English. The word *iho'iya:k'yanna* illustrates the translators' difficulty: *Iho* means to become a person and *iya:k'yanna*, to become mature. This construction indicates that first one must become a human being before thinking about maturing.

While important that Zuni be translated into English, it is urgent that all Zunis begin writing in their mother tongue, for it is the *Shiwi'ma Bena:we* morphology that can best connect the *A:shiwi* past to the present.

Corn Mountain/Pine Mountain
Following the Seasons

Dowa Yalanne/Ashek'ya Yalanne
Debikwayinan Idulohha

written by
Arden Kucate & Edward Wemytewa of Idiwanan An Chawe
and
Donna Porterfield & Ron Short of Roadside Theater

original music by *Ron Short*
choreographed by *Arden Kucate*
directed by *Dudley Cocke*

Cast

Idiwanan An Chawe	Roadside Theater
Arden Kucate	*Tommy Bledsoe*
Dinanda Laconsello	*Kim Neal Cole*
Edward Wemytewa	*Ron Short*

and five to sixteen dancers and singers. Regulars have included:
Christopher Edaakie, Francis Leekya, Jr., Jarvette Chopito, Vanita Besselente,
Kirk Romancito, Ivanna Romancito, Jerold Waikaniwa, Susan Mahooty,
Vaughn Awelagte, Keith Edaakie, Loren Ukestine, Ethan Wemytewa,
Elgin Hechiley, Charlene Hechiley, Demetrius Pinto, Kassie Kucate, Carleen Hustito,
Kayla Eriacho, Garrett Edaakie, John Niiha

Revealing a Zuni–Appalachia Collaboration

Entrance

(Zuni singers enter stage right, singing. Roadside then joins from stage left, and the two songs merge and become one.)

Kumanchi A:wan A:nakya *(song)*

Ya' e:...ya' e:ne:ya.
A:yo:...o:... ha:yowa: tsine:...
A:yo:...o:.... ha:yowa: tsine:...
A:yo:...o:...
Kuchimiya:...lu:... ahe:...ne:...ya.
Ya:he:lo.

Wings to Fly *(song)*

One day the Lord will come,
And give me wings to fly
Then my heart will soar,
And carry me over the mountains.

Kim

There are some who say the world is a machine.

Arden

Hame' a:benan, ulohnan ma:kinanne le'dikwe:'a.

Ron

There are some who say it is only a willer-the-wisp of our imagination.

Edward

Hame'a:benan, domt yanłi'dohan ikna' ho'n a:wan etts'a'kyatchoy'a.

Dinanda & Kim *(together)*

There are some who call it Mother.
Da: hame' Tsitda le'andikwe:'a.

Ukkwadonna

(Ashiwi denena:kw idokkwakwi ukkwado, denayna:wa. Roadside weshikk'yakwin ukkwadonan iwoslik'yanna, la:ls deyna: ihabonna, dobinde yo'ana.)

Kumanchi A:wan A:nakya *(denanne)*

Ya' e:...ya' e:ne:ya.
A:yo:...o:... ha:yowa: tsine:...
A:yo:...o:... ha:yowa: tsine:...
A:yo:...o:...
Kuchimiya:...lu:... ahe:...ne:...ya.
Ya:he:lo.

La'hinakya Ebisse:we *(denanne)*

Kya:k'i' ho'n a:wona:wil'ona' iynan,
Ho' la'hidun'on akkya hom ladenna
Les'hap, hom ik'e:nan ik'eyado:nan,
Lahn hoł adela:wa'kowa' yadelan allunna.

Kim

There are some who say the world is a machine.

Arden

Hame' a:benan, ulohnan ma:kinanne le'dikwe:'a.

Ron

There are some who say it is only a willer-the-wisp of our imagination.

Edward

Hame' a:benan, domt yanłi'dohan ikna' ho'n a:wan etts'a'kyatchoy'a.

Dinanda & Kim *(i:habona)*

There are some who call it Mother.
Da: hame' Tsitda le'andikwe:'a.

Ron
We make the earth by walking upon it.

Edward
We name the earth by talking.

Tommy
We celebrate the earth by dancing.

Arden
We honor the earth by singing.

All
Homeward Now (song)
Homeward now, shall I journey,
Homeward upon the rainbow.
Homeward now, shall I journey,
Homeward upon the rainbow.
To life unending and beyond it,
Yea, homeward now shall I journey.
To joy unchanging and beyond it,
Yea, homeward now shall I journey.

Edward
Good evening and welcome. My name
is Edward Wemytewa.

Arden
This is Dinanda Laconsello.

Dinanda
And that is Arden Kucate.

Ron
Hon ulohnanna'kowa' a:walluna' hon ulohnan ashna:we.

Edward
Beya:w akkya hon yam Awidelinne Tsitda shi'una:we.

Tommy
Yode:w akkya hon ulohnan an dewanan łana'
ashe:na:we.

Arden
Dene:w akkya hon ulohnan ayyułashshik'e:na:we.

Demł'ona
Yam Heshoda:kwi Ke:si (denanne)
Yam heshoda:kwi ke:si, si ho's a:nuwa,
Yam heshoda:kwin amidolanne akkya a:nuwa.
Yam heshoda:kwi ke:si, si ho's a:nuwa,
Yam heshoda:kwin amidolanne akkya a:nuwa.
Hoł dek'ohannan kwa' ibałdok'e:na'mankwi,
E:ha yam heshodakwin ke:si, si ho's a:nuwa.
Hoł isha'małde i:k'ettsanna' a:deyakwi,
E:ha yam heshodakwin ke:si, si ho's a:nuwa.

Edward
Ko'n don sunahk'yanapkya. Ma' awisk'wat don a:wikya.
Ho' Edward Wemytewa (Wi:maydiwa) le'shina.

Arden
Lu:kya Dinanda Laconsello (Lakonselo).

Dinanda
La:ł uhsi Arden Kucate (K'u:k'ahdi).

Edward

We are Idiwanan An Chawe, the Children of the Middle Place. Many years ago, when I was a teenager, I met Dudley Cocke, and over the years we have become friends. He introduced me to these friends from Roadside Theater, and they have been visiting Zuni for fifteen years, telling their stories and singing their songs. And we have been to Kentucky telling Zuni stories and dancing. Tonight, that's what we're going to do here together.

Kim

Keshshi. Ho' Kim Neal le'shina. Edward taught me that, but I guess I better speak Mountain instead. Hello, my name is Kim Neal. This is Tommy Bledsoe and Ron Short, and we are part of Roadside Theater from Whitesburg, Kentucky. And we're very happy and excited to be here in Zuni.

Dinanda

You might be wondering what we're doing here on this stage together.

Arden

Yeah, I've started to wonder that myself.

Ron

A few years ago, I met a German lady in Canyon de Chelly and I told her I was headed for Zuni . . .

Arden (*as German Lady*)

"Oh no, leibchen, don't go there. I have just come from Zuni and there is nothing there but dust and dogs, dust and dogs!"

Edward

Hon Idiwanan An Chawe. Dem ho' tsam ts'ana' ho' Dudley Cocke annabidikya. Emma debikwayips, hon i:kuwaye: ashkya. Da: an tse'makwinn akkya lukno Roadside Theater hon i:kuwaye:w ashnapkya, la:ł Shiwinakwin asdemłan apden yałdo' debikwayna' de'chi's yałashona: a:witdela. A:wiyna, yam delapna: a:beyenan, da: dena:w denena:we. Da:chi hon liłk'ont a:dey'ona' Kentucky'kwin a:wa:nan, kwa'hoł hon a:beyenan, yodibekkya. Lukkya' dehłinan, hon habona' lesnuna:wa.

Kim

Hello. My name is Kim Neal. Edward dey'ona' hom anikk'yakkya, lesn'apde el ana wan ho' yam ko'na adela'kowa hon a:beye:n'ona' ho' beyetdu. Keshshi. Ho' Kim Neal le'shina. Lukno Tommy Bledsoe dap Ron Short. Hon Roadside Theater'an a:dey'ona, hon Whitesburg, Kentucky'kwin a:wiya. Lił hon Shiwin'an dina' hon i:k'ettsannan da: hon ants'ummehna:we.

Dinanda

Ko'ch imat ley'ap ist don i:willaba' łuwayałdoye, honk'wat don le'n hoł i:tse'ma.

Arden

E:, ma' da: ho' deyande lesna' ho' tse'me:'a.

Ron

Ma's ko:wi' hoł debikwayi ke:si. Les a:na' Canyon de Chelly'an ho' Che:ma:kw okyattsik ashshu'wan ho' yam Shiwinakwin a:n'ona ho' adinekkya . . .

Arden (*Che:ma:kw Okyattsik yashna*)

"Dishshomahha holo, hom cha'le, eł do' isk'on a:namdu. Ho' chim Shiwinakwin iya. Istk'on kwa' kwa'hoł de'amme, domt luho: dap wattsida, luho: dap wattsida!"

Kim

But, strange as it may seem, there's something about Zuni that feels like home to us. Hillbillies and Zunis are a lot alike.

Tommy

Me and Edward was talking about how we growed up and we both agreed that

Edward

the best six years of our life were spent in

Tommy & Edward

first grade.

Edward

You heard about Zuni time? We show up an hour late. Them hillbillies show up three days late!

Dinanda

Yeah, even their luggage was four days late.

Tommy

Some folks say that hillbillies and Zunis both talk funny.

Edward

We don't ta' like dat.

Arden

They call tomatoes " 'maters."

Tommy

You all call mothers "mudders."

Arden

" 'taters"

Kim

Lesnapde, deyałatda: dophoł ikn'apde, imat Shiwin'an kwa'hoł de'on akkya hon k'yakweniy' ikna' hon ik'unnaba. Hillbillies dap A:shiwi ełt'hoł a:hi:nina.

Tommy

Edwardkwin hon yam ko'hoł leya' ko' leyhoł iho'iya:k'ekkowa hon beye:nan, hon habona' tse'map

Edward

dobalekk'ya debikwayina:w de'chi hish a:wali'kowa' hon

Tommy & Edward

firsh grade grade'an an utchu'kya.

Edward

Don ayyu'ya:naba, kwa' hoł yadokkya akkya a:wa:ne. A:shiwi, dobinde yadokkya idullapna' de'chi hon a:yaluk'e:a. Da:chi hillbillies a:dey'ona' ha'i dewap a:de'chinna!

Dinanda

E:ye, da: a:wan k'wapbo: a:deyande a:widen dewap a:de'chinna.

Tommy

Hamme' a:benan, hillbillies dap A:shiwi hawi:nina' bu'suna' a:beye:'a.

Edward

We don't ta' like dat.

Arden

Yam tomatoes, " 'maters" le'a:wandikwe:'a.

Tommy

Don yam a:tsitda, "mudders" le'a:wandikwe:'a.

Arden

(Yam k'yabi mowe) " 'taters"

Tommy
"brudders"

Dinanda
Enough of this! So here we are together, fixin' to tell stories, sing songs.

Kim
Now, we know that our stories are different.

Dinanda
Our songs are different.

Edward
Our language too.

Ron
Yes, our songs and language are different.

Arden
But we know the same rain falls in Kentucky.

Kim
The same sun raises its head ever' day over Zuni.

Edward
And every night the moon shines.

Dinanda
We grow corn and beans.

Tommy
We grow beans and corn.

Arden
We plant by the signs

All
and follow the seasons.

Tommy
(Yam a:baba) "brudders"

Dinanda
Lessi ke:si! Ma's hon lił deml'ona a:deyaye, hon delapna:w a:beyen diy'ha, da: denena:we' diyha.

Kim
Si hon ayyu'ya:naba, ho'n a:wa delapna:w a:doban holi.

Dinanda
Ho'n a:wan dena: a:doban holi.

Edward
Lesdik leya' ho'n a:wan bena:we.

Ron
E:ye, ho'n a:wan dena: dap bena: a:doban holi.

Arden
Lesnapde hon ayyu'ya:naba, uhsi'de lidokkya Kentucky'an lidobe:a.

Kim
Da: ko'n dewa:w uhsi'k'onde yaddokkya an oshshokkwin ichuk'oskuna' Shiwina'kowa yadele:'a.

Edward
Da: ko'na' dehlina: ya'onanne walolok'e:'a.

Dinanda
Hon miwe' dap bokya:we lene:na:we.

Tommy
Hon bokya:we dap miwe lene:na:we.

Arden
Kwa'hoł yu'hedona:w akkya hon doye:na:we

Demł'ona
Debikwayinan denna' hon daban dina:ne
(—delakwayyi, olo'ik'ya, miyashe:nak'ya, dap dehts'ina).

Zuni Spring
A:shiw A:wan Delakweyinna

Arden

In ancient time, there lived a people in the Middle Place. The valley was surrounded by many villages near and far. It was a time when the earth was moist and fertile. The old ones, feeble as they were, and the young ones too, they all had in their minds and hearts the devotion to raise crops. Their existence depended upon the blessings of the seed family which was rooted in the culture since the Time of the Beginning, when the people had emerged from the womb of the Mother Earth. Eagerly everyone anticipated the planting season. Spring would come to them.

Edward

Before the planting was done, in preparation, the people of the Middle Place ventured out. To the north towards Twin Buttes and Blue Bird mesas they went, looking for places where there were heavy silt deposits built by flash floods coming down from the canyons. Others would head out west to K'ya'na; still others to the south, Heyalo:kwi, the Place of Silt. The remainder of the people would seek lands to the east around Doy'a. These places of moist and fertile beds would be investigated, and all would eagerly await the planting.

Arden

When the time came, grains from the seed family would be planted, and during the sprouting, when the people, young and old, saw the wakening of the plants, their spirits lifted.

Arden

Ino:de. Idiwan'an łuwal'ap, lessi' dekkwin hame' łuwala:w ullapna'kya. Dem Awidelin Tsitda k'yahkwi ya:n'ap, a:deya'kya. A:lashshinde, a:waminande, ts'ana' deyande, kwa'hoł uwak'yanapdun'ona' che'k'wat isha'małde a:wan tsemakwi: deya'kya. Ko'n Chimik'yana'kowa, yam Awidelin Tsitda an ukkwaykowa' yam do:shonan łakwimo' adeyyaye. Akkya lesna' ants'ummehna' a:deya' delakwayikya.

Edward

Idiwan'an a:dey'ona lesna' yam kwa'hoł doyena:we' diyahnan kwa' dem hish doyena:kwin de'china'man a:ho' ukkwayilenna. Liwan'em bishl'ankwin ukkwayinan, Kwili Yalakwi, Łayaluk Yalakwin hołn hoł a'l akkwe'kowa heyalo: kwayina'kowa a:deshuna:wa. Isnok'on idehałna: awallunna. Hame' K'ya'nakwin hoł aweletchonna. Ham a:dey'ona liwan'em Ma'k'yayakwin dahna, Heyalo:kwin a:wa:nuwa. Da: ham a:dey'ona' dewankwin dahna' a:wa:na' Doya'kona' dehwa: deshuna:wa. Awekli:w a:k'okshin, da: a:dek'ina'kowa a:wawanaknan, sish chuw etch'amme' doye: ants'ummehna:wa.

Arden

Lesn adeya:.., ma's doye:na:kwin de'chip, yam dosho:we—do:sho: demłanahna—doyenak'yanna ke:si. Doyena'kya dap, lena: ukkwayip, ist a:ts'ana, a:ho' a:ya:na, ma' lesna yam shetda:we, bikya:we, chimdi: wiheya:w yo'ap, ma's che'k'wat a:ho'i a:wan tsemakwi: ik'eyadok'yanna.

Dinanda

As the corn, squash, melons, and all other seed varieties grew, each day they received encouragement. Thus, upon reaching a farming plot, one would greet, "a:wanikina:wa," and talk to the plants, the children. It was like that.

Ron, Tommy, & Kim
Following the Seasons *(song)*
The sun rises yellow in the eastern sky,
The northern light shines a ghostly white,
Southern skies burn red and bright,
As day slips into blue, black night.

And this old world keeps spinning round,
Sometimes up, sometimes down,
Summer, winter, spring, and fall
Following the seasons.

You drop four grains into each hole,
One for the squirrels and one for the crows,
One for the ground and one to grow,
'Til it's time for eating.

And this old world keeps spinning round,
Sometimes up, sometimes down,
Summer, winter, spring, and fall
Following the seasons.

Dinanda

Sheda:we, mo:deyała, melu:na, dap kwa'hoł demła do:shonan kwayipba, ko'n yado:w a:wanheshshik'yana:wa. Akkya lesna chuwhoł yam deyatchin'an de'chinan, yam lena:we, yam chawe, awannikinna. Lesna' a:deya'kya.

Ron, Tommy, & Kim
Debikwaynan an Haydoshna: Wotdaban Dina:ne
Dewankwin a'bo'yakwin yadokkya łupts'inna'
   ik'eyadok'ya,
Bishla'an k'ohannan k'eyat'ona walolo'a, haba ikna'
   lomomonne,
Alaho'an a'bo'yan allonaye, hish ashe: ko'n hoł ahonna,
La:ls yadon dehlinannankwin ili'adi, ik'widi.

La:ł luk ulohnan łashhina che'k'wat yallupcho,
Ishoł iyyamakkyana, ishoł manikkyana,
Olo'ik'ya, dehts'ina, delakwayyi, dap miyashe:nak'ya
Debikwaynan an haydoshna: wotdaban dina:ne.

Ko'n ak'o'kona' a:widen do:sho:w do' wopbenna,
Ohchi a:wan dobinde, k'walash a:wan dobinde,
Doba aweklan an dap doba ilena'dun'ona,
Kya:k'i' idoyna'dun dekkwi.

La:ł luk ulohnan łashhina idullapcho,
Ishoł i:yamana, ishoł manikkyana,
Olo'ik'ya, dehts'ina, delakwayyi, dap miyashe:nak'ya
Debikwaynan an haydoshna: wotdaban dina:ne.

Hairy Woman

Okyattsik Uhebałanne

Kim

There was a time, back in the old country, when people lived in tribes. There were Angles and Celts, Gaels and Picts. The tribes were always fighting. Always looking for more land to live on. Always in search of a new home.

Tommy

There's a story they tell about that time when there was a boat wreck and ever'body on it was drowned except one man.

Ron

This feller was lost and gave up any idea of ever findin' his way back to his people. He'd been months and weeks all by hisself. He come upon a deer, killed it. He's awful hungry. He looked around fer some place to build a fire and cook it, and find him some shelter, you see. He seen a cave not too far off, and he drug the deer over to it.

Tommy

The entrance to that cave was all wore slick like somebody

Kim

or something

Tommy

had gone in and out of it regular-like.

Kim

Kya:k'yan hoł ulohnan łashshin'an, dem a:ho'i' isamma: dana:w a:deya'kya. Angles dap, Celts dap, Gaels dap, Picts a:deyakya. Lukno isamma: dana:w isha'małde i:łade:napkya. Isha'małde ałna't dehwa:w a:deshuynapkya. Isha'małde dehwa:w chim'on' an ik'yakwe:nakya.

Tommy

Les a:na' delapnanne yokona' benan, imat k'yayanallukk'yanakya wakkwadop, ełthoł ansam upbo'kona' a:wakkwadopde, dobinde łashshik aniłłikya.

Ron

Uhs'ona' tsawak otdina'kya. Da: tse'mak dosakya akkya tse'map, kwa' elleya's kya:k'i' yam a:hame' ik'wałt a:wawashukwa. Ko:wi' hoł yachu:w dap duminku:w hish samma deya'kya. Hoł na'le' inkwin de'chinan, aynakkya. Hish osheman ashen iyahkya. Hoł aklunan, yam na'l akk'yatdun'ona' dehwan deshukkya. Da: hoł yam ik'yakwe:dun dey'an dehwan deshukkya. Imat yulotde hoł kya:k'i' a'l'oshden una'kya. Le'k'ons yam na'le' ełahan a:kya.

Tommy

A'l'osht'an, onan kwadon'an, hish k'yalolonne, chuw hołi

Kim

dahch'at kwa'hoł

Tommy

lubidenna kwadełnan, kwayilekkona' ikna'kya.

Kim

The man, he took some notice of this,

Tommy

but he didn't pay too much notice, 'cause he was plumb wore out from luggin' that deer around, so he just went on in.

Ron

Got him some sticks and got a fire started

Tommy

and commenced to broil that deer.

Ron

It was just about done, and all of a sudden right behind him he heared

Kim *(as Hairy Woman)*

a great big growl.

Ron

Looked around, and there stood a

All

great, big, hairy woman.

Tommy

Now let me tell you that feller was scared.

Kim

That woman must a-been seven

Ron

or eight foot tall, and she's a-standin' there with a deer throwed over her shoulder.

Kim

Tsawak lesna' duna'kya, les a:n' ayyu'ya:na'kya,

Tommy

lesna' duna'ende kwa' hish da: uhs'on hoł tse'manamkya, akkyap yam na'le ełahan iykow akkya hish yude'chinans, doms le'hoł kwadokya.

Ron

ławe' habok'yanans aklukya

Tommy

lesnans, na'le' shiyakłikya.

Ron

Shi'l akwan lesde:na', dekkwande, hish lem dey'an an mas'ande kwa'hoł hadiya:wap

Kim *(Okyattsik Uhebałan yashna)*

hish ashe: łeleledikya.

Ron

Yallu:bip, elaya

Demł'ona

hish le:' okyattsik uhebałan łana.

Tommy

Ma' lił do'na' ho' yadine, luk tsawak hish deshladikya.

Kim

Uhs'ona okyattsik hinik kwililekk'ya

Ron

dahch'at ha'ilekk'ya wekwin i:de'chin de'chi' hoł dashana'kya. Lesna' elaye, an chudi'kowa na'le yałdo' lesna' ela'kya.

Kim

She just stood there and looked at that man and looked at that fire. I don't reckon she'd ever seen a fire before . . . or a white man neither!

Ron

Well that man, he didn't know what to do. So he just reached over, pulled off a deer leg, and reached it up to that hairy woman.

Kim

She hesitated fer a little, sniffed at it, took a bite out of it, and then she gobbled that whole thing up in one bite.

Tommy

Then she tore a haunch off that deer she was carryin' and reached it over to the man to cook it.

Ron

Just as the white man was a-startin' to put it on the fire, he heared another growl,

Tommy *(as Hairy Man)*

a long, low growl.

Kim

Looked up and there stood the hairy man!

Ron

He knowed he was a goner fer sure!

Kim *(as Hairy Woman)*

But the hairy woman jumped on the hairy man and they fit and rolled over and over and fit. 'Til finally, the hairy woman killed the hairy man.

Kim

Lesna' okyattsik doms ela'kya. Uhsona' ottsi' andunadinan da: aklin uhsona' andunadikya. Ma' ho' tse'map, hinik kwa' kya:k'i' aklin hoł un'amme'kya . . . da: kwa' kya:k'i' hinik ho'i' k'ohanna' un'amme'kya!

Ron

E: ma' lukk'on ottsi' kwa' ko'hoł lewunakya an yu'he:t'amme'kya. Akkyas doms asyadonan, na'le' oyyihnan, uhsona' okyattsik ukna yadok'yakkya.

Kim

Okyattsik ko:wi' shokya'kya:.., musmunans, utdekya. Lesnans, yetch'am hoł uhsona' dapninde utdenan, hish demł ikwiłikya.

Tommy

Lesnan luk okyattsik yam na'le sedo'kow'annan oyyihnan, tsawak akk'yatdun'on akkya ukna yadok'yakkya.

Ron

Lesna's tsawak k'ohanna' chim hish akl'an yałdo'up, da: alna't doba łelelenan hadiya:kya,

Tommy *(Łashshik Uhebałan yashna)*

delana:na', la:łt uli'ma łeleledikya.

Kim

Dunak'eyado'up istk'ontde elaye, łashshik hish le:' uhebałan łana!

Ron

E:.. ma's ottsi' yam yałakwayidun'ona's ayyu'ya:na'kya!

Kim *(Okyattsik Uhebałan yashna)*

Lesn'apde okyattsik uhebałan dey'ona' łashshik uhebałan dey'ona' alla'hikya. A:ch i:wiyadenans, hish a:ch ashe: i:łakkya. Domt a:chi i:wideshnan, len'ep ibololoshkya. A:ch i:łada:... yalukwin okyattsik uhebałan dey'ona łashshik uhebałan łana' aynakkya.

Ron

So that feller, he just stayed on there at the cave. Finally, he just took up with the hairy woman, lived with her you know. When she'd go out a-huntin', she'd carry him out with her and set him on a log while she kilt the game and drug it back to the cave. He stayed there fer three years, and the hairy woman

Kim

she had a baby.

Ron

That feller, he'd stay at the cave and mind the baby. He was a-teachin' the baby and the hairy woman to speak his own language.

Tommy

Then one day five years from the time he'd got lost, while the hairy woman was out huntin', some people from his own country found him.

Ron

He knowed this was his only chance to get back to his own people, and he wanted to take his baby with him,

Tommy

but them fellers told him

Tommy & Kim *(as Fellers)*
"NO!"

Kim

"A half hairy baby would never make it in our country."

Ron

Akkya uhsona' tsawak dey'ona doms a'l'osht'an deya'kya. Doms okya' uhebałan illi' ideya:kya, den'at lesna, don ayyu'ya:naba. Okya' łada'kyan a:nan, yam ottsi sedo' kwayinnan, hoł k'ummannan animyałdo:nan, kwa'hoł wowe' laknan, doms yam a'l'oshdekwin a:wełahan a:nuwa. Lukk'on ottsi' ha'i debikwayina de'chi isk'on hoł okyattsik uhebałan illi' deya'kya

Kim

okya' chawashkya.

Ron

Tsawak a'l'osht'an chi imon, wiha ts'ana' ayyubatch'ap, da:chish okya' kwa'hoł demła k'yashima wowe ładekkya. Tsawak yam bena:w a:chiya annikk'ekkya.

Tommy

Kya:k'yan hoł dekkwande' deyadip, ma's otdikowa' apden debikwayip, tsawak an ulohnakwin a:ho' a:wiynan, awanapkya. Okya' uhebałan chi' łat'alluynan, kwa' im'amme'kya.

Ron

Ottsi' ayyu'ya:na'kya, hish i:nadin'amme' yam a:ho'i' a:deyakwin aksh a:nuwa. La:ł yam wiha ts'an il a:n iyahkya,

Tommy

lesn'apde a:wottsi' a:wiykowa' les'andikwekkya

Tommy & Kim *(A:tsawak yashna)*
"HOLO!"

Kim

"Lesna' wiha ts'ana' i:bachina' uhebałan deyan, kwa' ho'n a:wan ulohn'an ele dey'ushukwa."

Ron

He begged them to let him take the baby,

Tommy & Kim

but they wouldn't hear of it.

Ron

So they started out and got down to the boat. And as they's a-shovin' off, they heared a growl.

Tommy

They looked up

Kim *(as Hairy Woman)*

and seed the hairy woman a-runnin' towards them with her baby in her arms.

Ron

She waded in a-screamin', but the water got too swift and deep and she couldn't go no further.

Kim

She looked out towards that boat as it was leavin', and held that baby up over her head

Tommy

like she was a-sayin' fer him not to leave

Kim

"on account of the baby."

Ron *(as Man)*

That man, he was a-cryin' and a-motioning her to go back. Said he had to go . . .

Ron

Tsawak yam wiha ts'ana' il a:n iyahnan, hish di:shshomahha: bena:w akkya a:wambeyepde,

Tommy & Kim

kwa' an bena:w ihadiya:na:wammek'yandiyahkya.

Ron

Akkyas a:wa:nakkya akkya k'yayanallukk'yanakya k'yayakwin a:baniykya. Chimdi: wokk'yalin a:wa:nap, leleledip ihadiya:kya.

Tommy

Detduna yemaknan

Kim *(Okyattsik Uhebałan yashna)*

Okyattsik Uhebałan una:wap, yam wiha ts'ana' k'eshkwi' wokk'yalikwin ashe: ye:łan iykya.

Ron

Okya' ts'awawak'yan k'yan'an kwadokya, lesn'apde hish k'yap ts'ummen da: dedashan'ap akkya kwa's la:ł le'de kwadonamkya.

Kim

K'yayanallukk'yanakya a:nannankwin duna' yam wiha ts'ana' i:yamakwin anahk'eyado:kya

Tommy

"ełt do' a:namdu" le'anikwan ikna

Kim

"wiha ts'an an tse'makwinn akkya."

Ron *(Łashshik yashna)*

Tsawak k'oyende, okya ik'wałt a:dun'ona anhe:doshekkya. Tsawak yam i:nadin'amme' a:dun'ona beyekkya . . .

Kim

Then she let out a great big growl and tore that baby clean in two

Tommy

and flung one half out to the desertin' man in the boat

Kim

and a–huggin' the half what looked like her, turned away and walked back to the cave.

Turkey Dance

(Rattle shakes off stage. Turkey dancers and singers enter. The turkey is an important bird to the people. Its pelt is a prize to the kiva groups. The fast beat forces the dancers to pick up their heels, as they imitate the movements of the bird.)

(Turkey dancers exit.)

Rules of Zuni Storytelling

Edward

These are the Zuni storytelling rules. One, you want to make it easy for the storytellers. The encourager is "E:so." Let's try it: "E:so." An appreciative audience may be rewarded with additional stories.

Dinanda

Rule two, when the story ends with "Le:'semkoni'kya," you stretch like this to avoid becoming a hunchback in your young age. "Le:'semkoni'kya."

Kim

Isk'ons okya' hish ashe: leleledik'yanans, wiha ts'ana kwili dekkwin iyyapts'inan

Tommy

tsawak k'yayanallukk'yanakya akkya yokła'un'on inkwin yam i:bachikowa' an dobinde ibakukya

Kim

la:ł doba i:bachina, okya' ko'in'ona' hashin ik'eshkunan, yallupnans, ik'walt yam a'l'oshdekwin a:kya.

Dona Odanne

(Mas'an hoł chililidinna. Dona odi:kwe' dap denena:kwe ukkwadonna. Lukkya' wo'le, dona, hish a:ho'i' a:wan elekya. Kokko uba:wa'kowa hish an ba'in andeshemanak'ya. Heshshina' domdo'an'ona' akkya odi:kwe' ashe: a:wik'eyadoba, akkya doms luk wo'ts'ana ko' leye:n'ona ansummiyashan i:loshsha.)

(Dona odi:kwe ukkwayyinna.)

Delapna:kw A:wan Haydoshnanne

Edward

Lukkya delapna:kw a:wan haydoshna:we. Luk dobinde, chuwhoł dela:biyn'ona don ansatduna:wa, akkya kwa' yude'chishukwa. Don le'na' ansewashk'yana:wa "E:so." A:ma i:de'chunapshe, "E:so." Don elle yu'hadiya'k'yana:wap, ma' honk'wat chi alna't do'na' a:wan benuwa.

Dinanda

Luk kwilik'yanna:na' haydoshnanne. "Le:' semkoni'kya." Delapnan ya:'ap, don le'na' its'alina:wa. Akkya kwa' don ts'ana'de a:wik'ya'mo'shukwa. "Le:' semkoni'kya."

Turkey Girl

Dona E'lashdok'i

Arden

There was a time in the valley called the Middle Place. The valley was surrounded by many little villages—Hambassa:wa, Place of the Herbs; Binna:wa, Place of the Winds. One of the villages was called Mats'a:kya, where there lived a girl who raised and herded a flock of turkeys. Black turkeys.

Edward

Each day at sunup she went out of her small adobe home and released her children, the turkeys, from their pen. Then they would wander the valley heading south along the base of Dowa Yalanne mesa on to their feeding grounds. At noon they always worked their way around to the southern end of the mesa where there was a spring, Kyaki:m'a, a fresh water seep. The turkeys always enjoyed a drink of water during the heat of the day. Then her children would bed down to save themselves from the sun.

Arden

Late in the afternoon, the turkeys, accompanied by their mother, the girl, would resume their feeding around the foothills of the mesa as they headed back to their village of Mats'a:kya. By dusk, they would reach their pen and be let in to roost for the night. The girl would go into her adobe house, eat, and sleep. This would be another completed day, a day like any other.

Arden

Sonahchi, Son di: ino:de Idiwan'an a:deya'kya. Les a:na idulapna' łuwalapkya. Hambassa:w'a, Binna:w'a dap Mats'a:kya'a. Imat Mats'a:k'ya'an e'lashdok k'yakwe'kya. Yam dona a:willi' k'yakwe'kya. Dona a:k'winna.

Edward

Ko'n dewa:w hoł yam he:'ak'yak'w'an kwayinan, yam dona, an chawe, ukkwayik'yanan wowilli' allukkya. Ukkwayinan ma'k'yayakwi dahna, dewulli: łana'kowas idona: a:wa:nuwa Dowa Yala manikkya'kowa. Idiw'aps a:widulapna's Ma'k'yayakwin dahna Kyaki:m'an ik'yahkwishannan a:de'chinna. Isk'on dona lesna' hoł duduna:w elumanapkya dek'yalipba. An chawe's manikkya dełu'la'kowa iwo'yobanna.

Arden

Sunnaha: lesde:na' donas yam tsitda illaba idona: Dowa Yala' manikkya'kowa's ik'walts a:widullapnans, Mats'a:kyakwin a:wa:nuwa. Ashe: sunnahhaps, yam up'an a:de'chinna. An chawe' yam k'yak'wan ukkwadop, yan'ałdunna. Da:chish okya yams k'yak'wan kwadonans, idonan, iyude'chinahna:wa. Da:s luk yadon ye'le'kya. Le'na' ko'n dewa:w i:willap a:wallu.

Edward

One morning, as the girl was releasing her children from the pen, something unusual happened. At the main village of Halona:wa, the Sun Priest was summoning the villagers for a Ya:ya Dance to take place within four days. When the young girl heard the news, she became very excited.

Dinanda *(as Turkey Girl)*

"Oh! Perhaps I will dance! But first, I will ask my turkeys."

Edward

Because this would mean leaving her children for a day.

Arden

That morning, as usual, the girl and her flock continued to wander toward the south, where they would rest at the seep. All the while the girl thought of how she was going to ask the turkeys. The flock arrived at the spring and drank, followed by bedding down, as usual. There she decided to ask.

Dinanda

"Children, in four days there will be a Ya:ya Dance at the main village, and I want to go. I am looking forward to this, but you have to make the decision with me. You don't have to give me an answer right now, but this is to let you know what I am thinking. You will tell me tonight. I hope you will allow me to go."

Arden

By mid-afternoon, when the ground cooled off some, the turkeys left their bedding grounds and started to forage for seeds and fresh grass, all the time heading north back towards Mats'a:kya.

Edward

Imat lesna' a:deya' kya:k'yan hoł e'lashdok shamle kwayip, ko'hoł leyadikya. Imat Halona: łuwal'an Bekwin we'atchoy'a. A:widen dewap Ya:ya odipdun'ona' łuwala:w a:yu'ya:k'e:'a. E'lashdok hadiya:nan, hish k'ettsadikya.

Dinanda *(Dona E'lashdok yashna)*

"Oh! Hinik ho' odak'yanna! Lesnande wan ho' yam dona kela yayyałak'yanna."

Edward

Leha'ba yam dobinde yadon chawe a:yaknahanna.

Arden

Lehap shamle e'lashdok yam dona a:willi' ma'k'yayakwin dahna' a:wil idullapkya, ik'yahkwishannan, iyude'chinahnapdun'on akkya. A:wan tsitda da:chi yam yała'dun'ona' tse'mekkya. Ik'yahkwishan'an a:de'chinan, dudunan, iwo'yo'kya. Isk'on okya yała'kya.

Dinanda

"Hom chawe, a:widen dewap, łuwal'an Ya:ya odi:wa. E:t ho' a:n iyha. Ho' ants'umha. Lesnapde do'na ho' kela yayyałak'yan iyha. Wan eł ko'leya' hoł hom don adinena:wamme'du. Wan domt don i:tse'metdu. Hom don dehlap adinena:wa. Honk'wat hom don a:k'yana:wa."

Arden

Ashe: yasselak'yap, wetts'i' aweklan its'edip, dona yam iwo'yo'kona's debonbilaknans, kwa'hoł kyawe dap bek'yayu: idona:we. Bishlankwin dahna's Mats'a:kyakwins a:wa:kya.

Edward

The flock arrived at their pen, anxious to inform the girl of their decision. They settled in the pen as the girl came over to meet with them.

Dinanda

"Now, my children, what have you decided?"

Edward (as Turkey)

"Yes, our mother, we want you to enjoy yourself at the Circle Dance. You better go, for you have not visited your parents or friends in some time! However, you must keep in mind one very important thing, and that is to come back to us, your children, as soon as the sun falls low to the west. Can you promise us that?"

Dinanda

"Yes. I promise, my children."

Arden

Before she went back into her house, the flock told her that they had noticed her scratching her head all day long.

Edward

"Please sit down and bend over. It seems you have lice."

Arden

As soon as the girl bent over, the turkeys started pecking away at her scalp.

Arden & Edward (as Turkeys)

"Snap, snap, snap . . ." they rid her of the lice.

Arden (as Turkey)

"Now go in and wash your hair."

Edward

Dona yam k'yak'w'an a:de'chinan, yam ko'leyhoł e'lashdok ambenapdun'ona' i:tse'man shokyapkya. E'lashdok dinakwin iykya.

Dinanda

"Si hom chawe, hom an donsh i:tse'mekkya?"

Edward (Dona yashna)

"E:ye, ho'n a:wan tsitda. Do' Ya:ya oda'dun'ona dom an hon andeshemana:we. Chi' ele do' a:nuwa. Kwa' kya:k'i' do' yam a:łashshina:we, yam a:kuwaye, kwa' do' kya:k'i' a:washshu'w'amme. Lesn'apde, do' a:nande, eł delikwande, ho'na, dom chawe, do' a:wandommiyoshukwa. Chim yasselak'yap ik'wałt ho'na dinakwin do' iyanna. Do'sh le'na dey'unna?"

Dinanda

"E:ye, ho' lesnunna, hom chawe."

Arden

Yam k'yak'wan kwadonakya akkya a:nap, an dona imat hish yadonnilli oshshok isikłip unapkya. Akkya les'andikwekkya.

Edward

"Ma' wan a:ma i:mu. Ibowa'u, hinik do' mehkwi."

Arden

Isk'on a:wan tsitda ibowa'up, an dona oshshok dopdokya.

Arden & Edward (Dona yashna)

Sish domt dok'wak'wa'a. Mehkwishna: ya:k'yanapkya.

Arden (Dona yashna)

"Si łał kwadonan iwade."

Edward

The girl poured water into an old, traditional pottery bowl, and using a yucca root made a soapy lather. Now her long, black hair was very clean and shiny. Her turkeys remarked how pretty she was. They were happy for her.

Dinanda

"Oh, I have nothing to wear. I want to dance, but . . ."

Arden

Her children told her not to worry, to sit and wait.

Edward

The turkeys went off in every direction. Being supernatural creatures, they were prepared to meet the needs of their mother.

Arden

Directly, one of the big turkeys brought white buckskin moccasins and white buckskin wrappings for the leggings. Next, a large hen came in with a black robe-like manta dress, which would be draped around one shoulder of the girl, and a sash. Right behind her were two chicks dragging a white cape with red and black stripes. Last, necklaces—strands of turquoise and white shell beads—were brought by more turkeys. The girl was ready for the dance.

Edward

That night she was so excited it was hard for her to sleep.

Arden

Early the next morning, she let her turkeys out.

Edward

E'lashdok kwadonan, dowa sa'l'annan k'yalukya. K'yalunan, u'kwin hoł k'yaya:kya. Uhsona u'kwin ummo:w yokya. E'lashdok an daya:dashanna' sish a:wadena' walolonne. An dona lesdikwekkya, an i:k'ettsankya. Sish hiyowłushna' e'kokshi.

Dinanda

"Ma' e:t ho' odak'yan iyahnande, kwa' kwa'hoł ho' ulikya il'amme . . ."

Arden

Kwa' uhsona tse'manamdun'ona akya an chawe' doms shokya' i:mun hakk'yapkya.

Edward

An dona siwi'adikya. Dona yam k'yabin a:ho' a:dey'on akkya, yam tsitda ans kwa'hoł habok'yanapkya.

Arden

Lem dela:aps, dona łana uhsona dowa mokk'wa:w dap, kewullapna:w wopbona' yemaku. Da:chish dona hish le:' homłana' uhsona eha k'winna yadonan łeya' yemaku. Da:chish sabi:p a:chi ba'iykya kucha k'ohanna łeya' iykya. Yalu' li'akwa' dap alaho daku:we, uhs'ona' da: hamme' wopbonaba' a:wikya. A:wan tsitdas odakya ya:kya.

Edward

Uhsona dehłap e'lashdok hish k'ettsa: kwa' elle ałnamkya.

Arden

Dewap shamle, e'lashdok yam dona ukkwayik'yakkya.

Dinanda

"Children, today you will be out by yourself. Please don't stray off our usual way. I wouldn't want anything to harm you. I will return before sunset. I won't forget you."

Arden

Once the turkey flock left, the girl ran inside her hut to prepare.

Edward

She was ready in a jiffy. Turkey Girl was indeed beautiful! She started to walk to the village, only to find that she couldn't stop walking faster and faster. Soon she was running.

Arden

An alley in the main village led the girl to the central plaza where already, even in the early morning, it was crowded. The houses were stacked, some more than four stories high, all made of stone and mud bricks.

Edward

The dancing took place all day. Dance groups came and went after two or three songs.

Arden

Little boys and girls, teenagers, adults, and even elderly were dancing the Ya:ya. The men folk were partially naked around the torso and wore buckskin moccasins, ceremonial kilts, beaded necklaces, and colorful head-dresses. They were handsome.

Dinanda

"Hom chawe, don la:k'i' a:sam a:wallunna. Eł hish da: don le't a:wa:namdu. Kwa' akkya kwa' hoł do'na' ko'hoł a:wallewushukwa. Chim yado biyahhap, ho' iyanna. Kwa' do'na' ho' a:wandommiyoshukwa."

Arden

Isk'on an dona a:sam a:wa:nap, e'lashdok heshshina' yam k'yak'w'an yelahnah kwadokya. Iya:k'ekkya.

Edward

Lem delana:'ap, yelekk'yakkya. Hish e'l ihałuhn'amme. Okya's łuwalakwin a:kya. E:t kela yu'łahkun a:kya, hoł de'chip, hish yam ants'ummehan'on akkya, ye:lashna: dekwen a:ne.

Arden

Łuwal'an domma:na'kowa's bikwayinas, dehwitdo lanakwin de'chikya, hish ho'inaye shamle'de. K'yakwe: iyyałdopkya, hame' a:widen de'chi' hołi, da: he:awe' dap awe' akkya a:wona'kya.

Edward

Yadonilli' yodipkya. Yodip'ona dana: ukkwadełnan, kwili da:ch'at ha'i hoł denan ya:'ap ukkwayilekkya.

Arden

A:ts'ana' dap e:washdok dap a:tsawak dap a:ho'a:ya:na, chu'etch'amme' Ya:ya odipkya. A:wottsi' a:si'si'k'yayan, a:dowa mokk'waban, a:biłłaban, a:dakuban, da: hakdo: a:tso'ya' a:wulipkya.

Dinanda

The women were just as colorful in their buckskin moccasins, manta dresses, sashes, and colorful turquoise and shell necklaces. Contrasting with their long, black hair were multi-colored parrot feathers and yarn and bright ribbons in forms of huge blossoms. They were beautiful.

Arden

Amidst all the dancers was Turkey Girl, dancing hard and enjoying every moment of it. Her girlfriends were right beside her. But not for long, for soon the continuous dancing had taken the wind out of them. Not the Turkey Girl! She was lost in the rhythms.

Edward

By mid-afternoon, the flock of turkeys had worked their way back to Mats'a:kya, where they waited for their mother. There was no sign of her.

Dinanda

Not a sight. One of the older turkeys said to a pair of chicks . . .

Arden (*as Turkey*)

"Don't worry. Call out to her—perhaps she will come."

Edward

The chicks sounded off:

Dinanda, Arden, & Edward (*as Turkeys*)

"Kyayna: dok dok. Kyayna: dok dok. Ye:....., ka:chi: wu:li..., kyayna: dok dok, kyayna: dok dok, ye:....., huli, huli, dok dok dok dok."

Dinanda

Da: a:wokya lesna'dik a:tso'ya. Dowa mokk'wa: a:wuliban, ehhe: a:yadonan, e'nin dap li'akwa' dap ts'up daku: a:wulipkya. A:daya: k'win'ap, le'na'de a:wan oshshokkwi'kowa' mula lawe' dap chido:we, da: ałbiyahna:w akkya adeya: a:wona' lesa:wina'kya. Hish a:we'k'okshi'kya.

Arden

Odi:w'annan Dona E'lashdok'i, hish yam ko'n tse'man'ona odaye. Hish elum'a. An a:kuwaye illaba' yodiba. Delana:'ap, an a:kuwaye a:yude'ch'a. Holo, kwa' chi' Dona E'lashdok'i an ko'le'amme. Hish domdo'ap, ashenaye.

Edward

Idiwakya dap, da:chish dona danans ik'wałt Mats'a:kyakwin a:de'chinan, yam tsitda anshokya' dina'kya. Kwa' chuwhoł ettsa'kyadina'ma.

Dinanda

Kwa' chuw'holi. Kwa'dik hoł dona łana sa:bi:bi: les a:wanikwekkya . . .

Arden (*Dona yashna*)

"Eł i:tse'mana'ma. Ma' a:ma andeha:do:na:we— honk'watchi hadiya:nan iyanna."

Edward

Akkyas sa:bi:bi deha:do:napkya

Dinanda, Arden, & Edward (*Dona yashna*)

"Kyayna: dok dok. Kyayna: dok dok. Ye:....., ka:chi: wu:li..., kyayna: dok dok, kyayna: dok dok, ye:....., huli, huli, dok dok dok dok."

Arden

Now anxious, the turkeys decided to move towards Halona:wa in hopes of meeting their mother.

Dinanda

Their mother didn't come.

Edward

Back in the swirling dance, Turkey Girl was oblivious to the world, until something distracted her. Up on one of the highest roof tops was a solitary figure. The Turkey Girl called her girlfriends.

Dinanda

"Who is that young man? I want to dance with him!"

Edward (as Girlfriend)

"He is a son of a Rain Priest. He rarely comes out. He is very shy."

Dinanda

"Call him down for me. I will dance with him."

Arden

Soon the Rain Priest's son was dancing right beside the Turkey Girl. Now the spectators filled the sides of the plaza and the surrounding roof tops.

Edward

As the dancing had tired the girls earlier, now the priest's son, too, felt the exhaustion from the unending exertion. He wanted to rest, but the Turkey Girl insisted on one more, then another.

Arden

Kwa's el'ammap, akkya dona Halona:w łuwalakwin a:wa:kya. Honk'wat chi ist hoł yam tsitda anikdohna:wa.

Dinanda

Kwa' awan tsitda inamkya.

Edward

Da:chish Ya:ya odiw'an a:wan hish tsitda oda: ashenaye. Hoł isk'on kwa' hoł una:kya. Lak hoł imat chuwa hish samma elayal'ona' ank'ohak'yakkya. Yam a:kuwaye ishemakya.

Dinanda

"Chuwap uhsi la:k tsawak elayalaye? Ho' il odak'yanna!"

Edward (an Okya Kuwaye yashna)

"Uhsi Shiwan an tsawak'i. Kwa' hish kwayikwam ho'i, hish yatsa:willi."

Dinanda

"Hom an shemana:we. Ho' illi' odak'yanna."

Arden

Ko:wi dela:'ap, Shiwan an tsawak dap Dona E'lashdok a:chi i:willi odaye. Les'na' hish dehwit'an ho'inaye...Demaya:kwe dehwitdo'kowa dap deyala'kowa' łuwan idulapnaye.

Edward

Ko'na kela a:wokya a:yude'chikowa' lesna da: Shiwani an tsawak yude'chikya. Iyude'chinahan'iyhap, lesnapde Dona Elashdok kwa' ambikwe:n'amme balt'amme' oda'kya.

Arden

The turkeys had now moved to the outskirts of Halona:wa. They could hear the singing. For the second time, the chicks called out to their mother.

Dinanda, Arden, & Edward

"Kyayna: dok dok. Kyayna: dok dok. Ye:....., ka:chi: wu:li..., kyayna: dok dok, kyayna: dok dok, ye:....., huli, huli, dok dok dok dok."

Edward

They looked, but saw no one. Now the sun had fallen out of the sky, except for a sliver of light, the glow from the sun's crown.

Arden

The old turkey spoke angrily,

Edward (*as Turkey*)

"Let's go. Obviously our mother is not thinking about us. We will not go back to our home at Mats'a:kya. We will go towards the south, to those mesas and canyons across from Dowa Yalanne."

Arden

The flock moved quickly and deliberately away from Halona:wa. For the third time the chicks called out,

Dinanda, Arden, & Edward

"Kyayna: dok dok. Kyayna: dok dok. Ye:....., ka:chi: wu:li..., kyayna: dok dok, kyayna: dok dok, ye:....., huli, huli, dok dok dok dok."

Arden

Les hoł a:na' da:chish dona Halona:w łuwala bałdokwin hoł a:widiyułła'kya. Denap'ona' ihadiya:kya. Da:s kwilik'yanna:na' deha:do:napkya.

Dinanda, Arden, & Edward

"Kyayna: dok dok. Kyayna: dok dok. Ye:....., ka:chi: wu:li..., kyayna: dok dok, kyayna: dok dok, ye:....., huli, huli, dok dok dok dok."

Edward

Dona detdun'ap, kwa' chuw' holi. Le: hoł a:na' yadokkyas bani:kya, lesn'apde domt hish ko'n'apde yadokkya an hakin k'osk'ona walolokya.

Arden

Isk'on hols dona łana' ikyadikya,

Edward (*Dona yashna*)

"Si' anas a:wa:kya. Ma' imat kwa' ho'n a:wan tsitda a:wichemana'ma. Kwa' hon yam Mats'a:kyakwin a:wa:shukwa. Ma'k'yayakwin dahna isk'on yala:kwin hon a:wa:nuwa. Dowa Yal'an iwa'hipba."

Arden

Donas heshina' dapninde Halona:w'an dehwa:nap'kya. Da:s ha'ik'yanna:na' sa:bi:bi deha:do:nap'kya,

Dinanda, Arden, & Edward

"Kyayna: dok dok. Kyayna: dok dok. Ye:....., ka:chi: wu:li..., kyayna: dok dok, kyayna: dok dok, ye:....., huli, huli, dok dok dok dok."

Edward

The plaza was roaring with songs from many dance groups. Each seemed to be trying to out sing the other. It was the grand finale. Turkey Girl and the Rain Priest's son were hard at it, following a line of other dancers, working their way around the huge crowd. Then, suddenly, the Turkey Girl stopped, as if she had fallen into a trance.

Dinanda

"Hi:ya, my children!"

Arden

She ran out of the plaza, racing toward her turkeys.

Dinanda

"Wait, wait, my children!" The turkeys moved on as though they did not hear her.

Arden

Now Turkey Girl was losing ground because of all the weight she was carrying. First she dropped her cape, then she removed her necklaces. The sashes around her waist fell off. The leggings had to be gotten rid of. Finally, the manta dress had to be taken off. Now the girl was running freely after her children.

Edward

When the turkeys reached the base of Deshamikya Im'a mesa, they climbed. About half way up was a huge boulder where they settled. Here the turkeys, being supernatural creatures, imprinted their tracks in the stone. They looked back at the girl, who was now right behind them.

Edward

Dehwit'an hish domt ihaluhha, denena:kwe yam dena:w akkya iyyayyadona:we' diyha. Hish hiyo:lishna' odin łana. Dona E'lashdok dap shiwan an tsawak a:chi oda: ihaluhk'ya. Ho'inna'kowa a:chi idulla:bi. Dekkwande, Dona E'lashdok yam el'ande yushannadik'ekkya.

Dinanda

"Hi:ya, hom chawe!"

Arden

Dehwit'an ye:lahna kwayik'yakkya. Yam dona dinakwin a:wallahkya.

Dinanda

"Wanni, wanni, hom chawe!" Dona a:wa:kya, kwa' ihadiyana'man ikna.

Arden

Dona E'lashdok e:t ye:lahapde yam hashina kwanłeya:w ya:n'on akkya, kwa' iławedina'ma. Akkyas kela isk'on yam ba'in dap daku: kwiho:kya. Isnok'on e'nin ts'ulukda'kowa ikkwi'kowa' kwiho:kya. Kewullapna: yulishkya. Yalukwin yam ehha yadonan uhsona yulihkya. He:...chims yam eludeya' chawe a:wallahkya.

Edward

Lak hoł s Deshamik'ya Im'an a:de'chinans, adel'an a:yemakkya. Ya'l'an an idiwanashshi' a:yemaknan, a'le łana' al'an idinayałdo'kya. Yam k'yabin' a:ho' a:dey'on akkya isk'on ide'ana:napkya. Isk'on dona detdunadip, a:wan e'lashdok yaluye.

Arden

The older turkey spoke again to the flock,

Edward (*as Turkey*)

"Here she comes, lice and all. Si, (now), we will not be living like we have been. Our mother did not think about us. From now on we will roam the earth of our own free will. It will be like this. My little ones, sound out to your mother for the last time."

Dinada, Arden, & Edward

"Kyayna: dok dok. Kyayna: dok dok. Ye:....., ka:chi: wu:li..., kyayna: dok dok, kyayna: dok dok, ye:....., huli, huli, dok dok dok dok."

Edward

The turkeys flew, łaba:n . . .

Arden

Today, the rock from which they flew is called the Place of the Turkey Tracks.

Dinanda

This happened in ancient time.

Dinanda, Arden, & Edward

Le:' semkoni'kya.

Fiddle tune

"Fly Around My Pretty Little Miss"
(*The cast dances a Kentucky Running Set.*)

Arden

Isk'on kwa'dik hoł dona łana' leskwekkya,

Edward (*Dona yashna*)

"Da: wenan ist iyya, mepbon ts'ana. Si, kwa's hon yam ko'n a:deya'kowa hons a:deya'shukwa. Ho'n a:wan tsitda kwa' a:wan tse'manamkya. Hons lił a:la'hina' hons iwohhayak'yanna. Ulohna demła hon a:walluna. Si, hom chawe, luk alna't yam tsitda andeha:do:na:we."

Dinanda, Arden, & Edward

"Kyayna: dok dok. Kyayna: dok dok. Ye:....., ka:chi: wu:li..., kyayna: dok dok, kyayna: dok dok, ye:....., huli, huli, dok dok dok dok."

Edward

Donas łaba:n....a:la'hikya.

Arden

Da:chish a'l'annan ide'ana:napkowa' akkya la:k isk'on "Dona A:de'ana:wa" le'deshhina.

Dinanda

Ino:de Mats'a:kya'an łuwal'ap, le' leyadikya.

Dinanda, Arden, & Edward

Le:' sem koni'kya.

Tsiwiyyanashnakya łinłinan (Fiddle) denanne

"Fly Around My Pretty Little Miss"
(*Chu'w etch'amme' Kentucky a:wan odan yodibanna.*)

I Grew Up on a Farm

Ho' Kwa' Hoł Idoyena' Łakya

Kim

Whew! That'll keep you in shape won't it! I always did love to dance. From the time I was just a little bitty thing I was dancing with ever'body and anything. Now, some folks don't like to dance much. They say it's too much like work. Well, I tell you, I've done both, and I know the difference.

I grew up on a farm. It was the same farm that my family had lived on as far back as anybody could remember. It wasn't such a big farm, but it was big enough to keep my grandpa and grandma, Uncle Henry, Aunt Myrtle, their six girls, my mama and daddy, my brother and me, twenty milk cows, however many pigs was born that year, a bunch of chickens, a passel of barn cats, and a dog.

We grew ever'thing we eat and ever'thing our animals eat—and done most ever'thing by hand too—plowing with mules, hoeing and harvesting, cannin', pickeling, and drying ever'thing that could be canned, pickeled, and dried, bakin' our own bread from the wheat we grew, and washin' clothes on the wash board. And all them clothes had to be ironed. My grandma taught me to iron when I was eight. She'd say, "When you're done with that sheet, young lady, I don't want to see a single wrinkle in it. Don't give it a lick and a promise, girl, do it right the first time!" Well, we went to bed early of a night, and we went to bed tired.

Kim

Hahwah! Ma' le'na' akkya do' łun bissek'yanna, holoni! Che'k'wat isha'małde ho' yode: elumakya. Lak'yande'ma dem hish ho' lemshok ts'anande dens chuwanhoł dap dens kwa'hoł ho' a:willi' yodekkya. Le:w a:na' hame' kwa' yodiba: elumana:wamme. A:benan hish emma i:kwa:ni:we le'dikwe:'a. Ma' do'na ho' yadinetdu, ho' kwilide lesnukya, akkya ho' ayyu'ya:na kwa' a:ch hawi:nin'amme—oda: dap i:kwa:ni:we.

Deyatchiw'an heshshoda:w'an k'yakwe'an ho' deyachina:wan iho'iya:k'yakkya. Uhsi'de deyatchina:wan hom a:łashshina:w ko:mash ko'na' delana:na' a:deyaye. Kwa' hish da: deyatchinan łan'amme'kya, lesn'apde yu'de'chi' łan'on akkya lukno:kwe' ele a:deya'kya. Hom nana dap, hotda dap, kyamme Henry dap, tsitda łashshi Myrtle dap, a:chiya' dobalekk'ya ewe. Da: hom tsitda dap, datchu dap, baba dap, ho:o. Da: kwilik'yan asdemła a:kwik'yashnakya wa:kyashi dap, dens ko:wi'hoł bitsu:di a:chawokowa' dap, ko:wi'hoł doko:ko dap, mu:sa dap, dobinde watsida.

Demła hon yam kwa'hoł idoyna:w'ona hon lenenapkya, da: kwa'hoł demła ho'n a:wan wowe idoynapkowa—da: yamde asi:wakkya, hon kwa'hoł demł i:kwa:nik'e:napkya—mu:l akkya dets'ishe:napkya, łalle:napkya da: miyashe:napkya. Kwa'hoł dewalolo:w akkya wopba:wo'anna, dahch'at k'ya'obi:wan wopbobanna, dahch'at a:k'usk'yanak'yanna. Hon yamande yam kyawashnapkowa' akkya hon muwashe:napkya, da: he'k'yaba' nidelann akkya hon yam asi:w akkya kwanłeya: wok'oshoynapkya. Da: demła kwanłeya: a:tsałchonak'yanna. Ho' ha'ilekk'ya

We worked hard, but we never worked alone. Families and neighbors would go to each other's farms to help with the work . . . in the spring, fer the cleanin' and the plantin', in the summer fer the cannin' and the hay makin', and in the fall fer the butcherin' and the harvestin' of the crops . . . and at the end of the seasons, when the work was done, we had socials where ever'-body from all around got together fer a dance. We'd clean up and put on our best clothes, fresh off the clothesline, so starched and pressed we rustled when we walked. We'd all gather in a meadow that smelled of new mowed hay.

There'd be plenty of food to eat—Irene Seibert's coconut roll, Beulah Thompson's spice cake, Ella Crim's tea rolls, ham, deviled eggs, potato salad, apple pie, peach pie, cherry pie, chocolate pie, green tomato pie! Apple cider in the fall and iced tea in the summer.

We'd eat all that good food then set a while to watch the sun go down over the other side of the mountain. Directly, the music would ring out, and we'd dance. Old folks, young folks, children, anybody that had any wind in 'em at all would flat foot it, dance the reels, and waltz across that meadow in the moonlight as long as the fiddle and banjer players held out. When the last dog dropped, we'd start home, headed fer bed, with Sunday morning, milkin', and church just a few hours away. We was tired alright, but it was a different kind of tired.

debikwayik'yap, hom hotda its'ałcho: anikk'ekkya. Hom le'anikwanna, "E'le, do' uhsi bewi yałdon ya:k'yap, kwa' dobint dey'an dapde hoł kets'alin deya'shukwa. Kwa' dobinde kets'alin dapde ho' unakna'man iyha. Ełt dom do' ko'n'apde lesnu: beye:namdu, do' i:nadin'amme dapnimt a:na' eledey'unna!" Ma' dehł'ap shamle'de hon yam bewi:wa'kowa' iwo'yobekkya, hon ashe: ko'nhoł a:yude'china' iwo'yobekkya.

Hon ashe: i:kwanik'e:napkya, lesnapde kwa' kya:k'i' hon a:samma i:kwa:nik'e:nawamme'kya. K'yakwenuli: dap yadona:kwe' le'n'ep i:yansatdena: a:wallukkya . . . delakwayip, dek'okshenan, doyena:wa, olo'ik'ya kwa'hoł dewanna'kowa' wopba:washnan, da: hapbowa:washna:wa, lał miyashe:nak'yap wowe' łaknaknan kwa'hoł lena: yokona' habełk'yanak'yanna . . . le'na' debikwayinan an i:kwa:ni:w haydoshna: ibałdo'kya dap, i:kwa:ni: yele'kya dap, a:ho'i i:wik'oshk'yanaky akkya demła dekkwin habełnan, yodibanna. Hon ik'oshonan, ihandaklishna:wa. Hon yam kwanłeya:w a:k'okshi' bi'yał'an woya'ona wohanahnan, yulena:wa. łakyatdo:w k'yaw akkya ts'ałchona'kowa akkya hon a:wa:nap, domt ławawa'anna. Chuw' etch'amme' hoł dewuł'et'an chim beyahna'kya dey'an hon habonna. Chim beyahna'kon ikna' dechinnallunna.

Emma idonakya deyak'yanna—Irene Seibert an coconut mulo: chikwa bololo:we, Beulah Thompson an spice mulon chikwa, Ella Crim an ha:k'yawe' dudunan idonakya mulo: chikwa, bitsu:di shiwe, doko:ko mowe hekk'i:we, k'yabimow'annan kwa'hoł i:ya'sena, kwa'hoł kepbo' mulo: chikwa,—mansana, mo:chikwa, cinuwe:la, choklat, k'e:ts'ido'kya a:li'anna! Miyashe:nak'yap mansana k'yaleyabanna, lesnan olo'ik'ya ha:k'yawe'annan łek'yaya:w wokk'yali' a:wo'anna.

Nobody back home farms much anymore. Oh, we might put out a little garden, but we don't really farm. Most folks has some kind of time clock job, or no job at all. And there's them that's on the government draw. I got me a job. Two jobs really, 'cause it seems like I put in my eight hours, then go home and start workin' all over again. And, buddy, I'm on my own when I'm doin' it too. Sometimes my housework gets done, sometimes it don't. Now, I got a whole lot of things we didn't used to have when I was a kid—like a car and a TV, and a brand new, heavy duty, eight-cycle G.E. automatic washing machine 'cause I sure don't one bit miss washin' clothes on that wash board! And praise the Lord for permanent press, is what I say! There's some things I don't want to go back to.

Kwa'hoł ido:w a:walideya' habokowa' hon idonan, le'n'em yala:kwin yadokkya yadop, hon unaba' dinak'yanna. Les a:na denan kwayip chims hon yodibanna. A:ho' a:ya:na, chim'on a:ho'i, a:ts'ana, chuw' etch'amme a:na dets'um'ona doms tsodede'anna, wekwi: ch'apch'a'anna, simon alluna' yodibanna, da: i:k'eshkwiba, yu'łahk'una' yodibanna. Ya'on'ap, beya'kowa yodena: wohhayak'yanna, che'k'wat chi' kya:k'i' linłik'yana:kwe dechunedun dekkwi. Dem kya:k'i' wattsit hish yude'chi:w akky a:lanip, chims hon yam k'yakkwin a:wa:nuwa, yam bewikwin a:wa:nuwa. Lesnande domt ko:wi delana:'ap, shamles wa:kyashi a:kwik'yashnak'yanna, da: Duminku o'anna. Hish hon a:yude'chinak'ekkya, lesnapde doban hoł yude'chi: deya'kya.

La:k'i' hon k'yakwen'an kwa's chuwhoł deyatchi:w dap wowe' i:kwa:nik'e:na'ma. Hay ma' is'hoł hon yam dekwan'an ko:wi' doyenna, lesnapde kwa's hish da: hon deyatchi:washe:na:wamme. Em'ona kwa'hoł i:kwa:ni: illaba, yadokkya idullapna' andabann a:na' i:kwanik'e:na:we. Dahch'at kwa' kwa'hoł i:kwani:w illa:wamme. Da: lał ham a:dey'ona Washindo:w'on'an dewuko'liya: he:dishe:na:we. Ho' i:kwa:ni: illi. Hay ma' kwili lesde:na akkyap ho' ha'ilekk'yan yadokkya idullapna' ho' i:kwa:ni:w elekk'yanan, yam k'yakkwin de'chinan, doba i:kwa:ni banan kwayik'yanna. Kuwaye, hish ho' samma yamande ko'hoł leyenna. Is'hoł ho' yam k'yakw'an i:kwa:ni:w yelekk'yanna. Is'hoł kwa' yele'shukwa. Ts'anan kwa' yam kwa'hoł il'amme'kona's la:k'i' ho' emma kwa'hoł illi—shiwayan dap, iwopba'nakya łelonne, da: kwanłeya: wok'oshonakya chim'ona, hish ts'umme, ha'ilekk'ya cycle G.E. automatic. Leha'ba kwa' la:ł ana he'nidelann akkya ho' kwanłeya: wok'osho: tse'mana'ma! Ma' awisk'wat da: ho'n A:wona:wil'on an tse'makwin akkya da: permanent press, ho' le'kwe:'a! Isno kwa'hoł a:deya'kona' kwa' ana ho' ik'wałt a:wandeshemana'ma.

But there's some things I miss too. I ain't been to a social in many a year. Ever'thing's changing so much and so fast, it can make you feel like you're out in some briar patch a-lookin' fer yourself. *(pause)* I guess for me though, it just comes down to the fact that I've danced by myself in my living room to the music comin' out of the radio, and I've waltzed across the meadow with folks that's dressed fer the occasion, and I know the difference.

(Folds into "Margaret's Waltz," played on the fiddle.)

(Corn dancers enter and stand upstage.)

Lesnapde da: isnhoł kwa'hoł ho' a:wayyu'a:sh'a. Kwa's emma debikwayina ho'i' i:wik'oshk'yanakya habon'an ho' yakshuna'ma. Hish łubidenna' emma kwa'hoł i:yallishan a:nap, do' otdinay ikna' mok'yachibana'kowa' do' ideshun allunna. *(Wan lil ko:wi' chun'anna)* Ma' ho' tse'map, ho' moła' beye:'a, yam k'yakwe delit'an denakya łelonnan denaban'on akkya ho' samma yodekkya. Da: dewuł'etdo'kowa' chuwanhoł odenakya akkya a:kwanłeya: k'okshi' ho' a:willi' yoden le'n'em iwa'chokkya. Akkya ho' ayyu'ya:na, kwa' hawi:nin'amme.

(Lils "Margaret's Waltz" kwadonna, tsiwiyyanashnakya linlinan ts'an' akkya.)

(Miwe' A:woda:na:kwe' ukkwadonan, iluwayałdok'yanna.)

Village Women Enjoy Dancing
Łuwal'an A:wokya Yodiba: Elumana:we

Dinanda

Village women enjoy dancing. My mother danced the Harvest Dance when she was little. When the dance was over she was tired but had good feeling, clear mind, and was happy. She looked forward to such celebrations, not only for the dancing, but for the opportunity to be with the village women to prepare the harvest feast.

When a dance was scheduled, people would gather. My mother would join the activity with her folks, relatives, and friends. They would come together. One danced or one was a spectator. People participated by watching. This dancing and spectatorship was what my mother looked forward to. She grew up with this.

Today, when there is something like that in the village, the people still gather. At a big celebration, women—the old and the young—happily join in the activities. Everybody pitches in. They do things together because they are teaching each other. So when something is happening, *who is responsible?* It is these women folk! Cold or rain, they bake bread or cook stew. Because of these women folk, festive food gets done. They help to meet the traditional ways of the village. We women are involved in meeting the religious obligations.

I talk about women, and at the time of winter festivities, when the people cook together, grinding corn, everyone looks forward to it. Before the actual day of the grinding, there is preparation. Mano and metates are gathered. Corn is crushed.

On the day of the corn grinding, during the late afternoon or evening, women and the villagers gather with

Dinanda

Luwal'an ma' a:wokya yode: elumana:we. Hom Tsitda dem ts'anan, lesna Sade'chi: yodekkya. Oda: dechun'ap yude'chinande, che'k'wat an tsemakwi:w mola'kya, an tsemakwi:w k'okshi'kya. Hish k'ettsankya. Le'na' dey'on akkya odipdun'ona', dap ido:wo'annuwap, ants'ummeshekkya.

Odi:wannuwap, a:ho'i habonna. Isk'on hom tsitda yam a:lashshina:w dap, i:yanikina:w dap, a:kuwaye a:wunak'yanna. I:willap ihabelenna. Dop'am hoł demayak'yanna, da:ch'at dop'am hoł odak'yanna. Yodibap, demayadinak'yap, uhs'ona' hom tsitda hish ants'ummeshekkya. Le'n iho' iya:k'ekkya.

La:k'i' lesna' ko'hoł luwal'an leyadinnuwap, dem lesna' a:ho'i ihabele:'a. Kwa'hoł łana deyadinnuwap, a:wokya —a:lashshinde, a:ts'anande—kwa'hoł'anna'kowa' a:yu'anikdo' iwoslibe:'a. Yanse'liyashshe:'a. Che'k i:willaba' ko'leye:na:wa, akkyap da: kwa'hoł i:yanikk'e:na:we. Akkya kwa'hoł łana deyadinnuwap, *chuwap ma'i?* Ma' ima luknok'on a:wokya! Dets'apde, lit'apde, mulo:na:wa, da: woleye:na:wa. Luknok'on a:wan tse'makwinn akkya łana' dewap, ido:w yelebe:'a. A:wan tse'makwinn akkya, ho'i' demł an haydoshna:w yelebe'a. Le'na' a:wokya' wosli' kwa'hoł dewusu' haydoshna:w imołabe'a.

Lukn a:wokya ho' a:wandepbe. Dehts'ina emma yode: haydokwin de'chip, lesna ho'ikya i:willap ido:w'ap, oknak'yap, chuw etch'amme' ants'ummeshe:na:we. Dem ko:hoł dewa:w etchikwin kwa'hoł demdeyandes yelekk'yabanna. Ak'e:w dap yali:w habelanna. Chuwe' sak'o:w owo'anna.

enthusiasm. When the song starts *(drumming begins)*, grinding begins. Corn grinding is done with joy and with ease. The corn grinders—girls, women, and older folks—cleanse their minds and hearts. They are happy in each other's company. They are attentive to each other. There is eating and dancing. There is talking—clans, households, everyone for that time becomes one people. Everyone is of one mind. When this happens, let it be, for we are happy.

When there is work to be done, why shouldn't we celebrate?! We look forward to it because at the time of the Emergence, when we came out of our Mother Earth, we received a gift. We were blessed with the seed family, and the people are protected by them. Also, when we talk about the flesh of the seed, who will be among us forever, they too are in the form of women; we are talking about our spiritual children, the Corn Maidens.

Corn Maiden Dance

(In the winter fasting period, the Corn Maiden family of seeds are guarded and lullabies are sung to them to ensure that they rest like babies. The dance is the rocking of the babies.)

(Corn Maiden dancers exit.)

Ron, Tommy, & Kim
Following the Seasons *(song)*

The corn grows green
And the corn grows tall.
The sun shines down
And the warm rains fall.
New life springs from the old,
It's something to believe in.

And this old world keeps spinning round,
Sometimes up, sometimes down,
Summer, winter, spring, and fall
Following the seasons.

Oknak'yannuwaps, sunhapba dahch'at dehl'apba, a:wokya dap hame' łuwal'ona' a:yu'anikdo' habelanna. Denan kwayips *(dese'anapba)*, deyadinna. Eludeya' oknak'yanna. Okna:kwe—e:washdok'i, a:makk'i, a:ho' a:ya:na—i:yan tsemakwi: dap ik'e:na:w k'okshuna:wa. Ma' k'ettsannishshi' i:willaba' a:deyak'yanna. Iyyayyułashshik'yanna:wa. Idonak'yanna da: yodibanna. I:yashshu'wadinak'yanna—annodi:we, k'yakwenuli:we, habon'ona' wans dobint a:ho' awiyo'anna. Dobinde tse'makwin illabanna. Le' leyadip, chi' ele lesnadi, hon i:k'ettsananna.

Lesna' i:kwa:n'annuwap, kop ma' la:t hon kwa' ants'ummehnapshukwa?! Hon ants'ummehna:wa, leha'ba chimik'yanak'yap, yam Awidelin Tsit'annan hon ukkwayip, ho'na' yanitchiya'kya. Do:shonan demłanahna' ho'na' yanitchiya'kya, akkya a:ho'i' a:dehya. Akkya hon a:shi'na ya:naye. Ma' uk'wat ist ho'n a:wan dowa shi'na:w a:bik'ya' a:deya'dun'ona' dem da: a:wokya, K'yabin A:ho'i—A:dow E:washdok'i.

Miwe' A:wodabanna

(Dehts'ina a:deshkwibap, A:dowa E:washdok a:wayyubatchidinak'yanna, wiha ts'an ikna' a:wandenabanna akkya iyude'chinahna:wa. Luk odan miwe' a:dałnak'yanna akkya a:ho'i yanitchiyak'yanna.)

(Miwe' A:woda:na:kwe' ukkwayinna.)

Ron, Tommy, & Kim
Debikwaynan an haydoshna: wotdaban dina:ne.

Shetda: ashenan ilenak'ya
La:l shetda: a:dasha'a.
Yadokkya an dek'yałnan baniyu
Da: lidokkya a:yusu a:baniyu.
Kwa'hoł a:łashshina'kow'annan chim'on a:wiyo'a,
Hish lukkya' iłdemanakya.

La:l luk ulohnan łashhina idullapcho,
Ishoł i:yamana, ishoł manikkyana,
Olo'ik'ya, dehts'ina, delakwayyi, dap miyashe:nak'ya
Debikwaynan an haydoshna: wotdaban dina:ne.

Zuni Summer
Shiwin'an Olo'ik'ya

Arden

In the summer, the Uwanami, Keepers of the Rain, would release the clouds to the people. When the clouds bellowed up into the sky, the feelings of the villagers rose in joyous anticipation.

Edward

As they raced to their fields, the thunder clouds burst. The old ones, though they may have seemed feeble a short while earlier, weren't. No! During the downpour, like ants, they scurried about making small diversion channels. What little amount of rain that fell was collected. The plants grew willingly.

Arden

Raising a crop means dealing with a number of things like skunks, porcupines, raccoons, and sometimes deer, all critters who like to eat tender plants. Other times, it is the grasshoppers and birds. With this understanding, the people humbled themselves to the animals, the birds, and the insects.

Arden

Olo'ik'ya, lesn hoł a:deyakwin Uwanami lo:kwayik'yana:wa. Łido'dun'ona akkya lo'l'imt'ap, łuwal'ona' a:wan tsemakwi:w ko'kwa dewuchinak'yanna.

Edward

Ma' lesna yam deyatchi:wan hoł a:de'chip, awełuya:w a:wiyan'ona' a:kwachip, ist a:łashshinde, a:wamin iknande, ełła, kwa' a:wamina'shukwa. Hish łidokkya shiwuwu'ap, hal ikna' domt i:k'ya'shetchonna' akkwe:w a:ts'an a:washna:wa. Ko:wi' łido:w k'yawe' yokowa habełk'yana:wa. Lena: yu'anikdo' a:ła'anna.

Arden

Dem da: deyatchina'an kwa'hoł uwak'yap, deni'kya. Leha'ba kwa'hoł wema:we dap wowe — subik'o, chibi, we:dasha, is'hoł nawe, lena:w uwa'an'ona' idona:wa. Dahch'at is'hoł chapba dap, wots'ana:we. Lesna yam ayyu'ya:nap'on akkya a:ho'i' dikwahna'dun'ona' wema:we dap wots'ana:we dap noma:we a:wanbeye:napkya.

Edward

"Yes, go ahead and eat to your heart's content. However, do not allow yourself to do any damage. Leave some so there will be something left to ripen. Eat and be on your way," they would say.

Dinanda

Yes, the people used to talk to the animals, too.

Edward

"Eye, ma'chi ele don yushelk'yanakwin idona:we. Lesn'apde, eł hish da: don ido:w ko'di: lewuna:wamme'du. Ko:wi' hoł etchuna:we akkya uhs'ona' lena:w a:łashanna. Ma' idonan łun a:wa:she," a:ho'i' le'dikwekkya.

Dinanda

Ele:de, les a:na' a:ho'i' wema:w a:washshu'we:napkya.

Jack and the Animals
Jack dap Kwa'hoł Wowe

Ron

Don't you know, there was a time when animals and people could talk.

Kim

They still can talk . . .

Ron

Yeah, but not to each other.

Tommy

Maybe if we listened real close, we could.

Ron

I don't know, but I do know there was a boy who lived in the mountains who could talk to animals. His name was Jack.

Tommy (as Jack)

"Howdy, my name is Jack."

Kim

Now Jack and his family was poor people, had to raise ever'thing they eat. So they couldn't afford for the animals to be eating up ever'thing.

Ron

But Jack had listened real good and he could talk to animals, so he went to 'em and told 'em,

Ron

Don ayyu'ya:naba, imat kya:k'i' e:t kwa'hoł wowe dap a:ho'i' i:yashhu'we:napkya.

Kim

Ma' e:t dem i:yashshu'wapdun'ona . . .

Ron

Ehha, lesnapde kwa' i:yunakkya a:beye:na'ma.

Tommy

Ma' honk'wat hish hon eledokna' yu'hadiya:k'yana:wap, elek'yanna.

Ron

Ma' i:me, da:chi luk ho' ayyu'ya:na imat lak hoł yala:w'an tsawak k'yakwe'kowa kwa'hoł wowe' a:washshu'wekkya. Jack le'shina'kya.

Tommy (Jack yashna)

"Keshhi, ho' Jack le'shina."

Kim

Les a:na Jack dap an iyyanikina: a:dewuko'liya'kya, kwa'hoł yam idonakya yamande a:łak'e:napkya. Kwa' a:wan iho:t'am'on akkya kwa'hoł wowe' dap wema: ido: a:wan'ibe:napkya. Kwa' kwa'hoł demła idona:wamme'dun'ona akkya.

Ron

Lesnapde chi Jack hish elle hadiya:wekkya akkya kwa'hoł wowe a:washshu'wekkya la:ł dinakwin a:nan lesa:wanikwekkya,

Tommy

"Look here, you critters, you can't be eating the seeds we plant or the corn 'fore it gets ripe or we'll all starve to death. You wait 'til it's harvest and I'll see you get fed plenty."

Ron & Tommy

So they made a deal.

Kim

And it worked out purty good.

Ron

But now, you know them Zuni critters, they couldn't help stealing some 'ever now and then. Hit's their nature.

Kim

In the same country there was this King and he had ever'thing, just about, that anybody could ever wish fer.

Ron

But, he got to thinkin' what he really wanted was a grandson, somebody to leave his kingdom to.

Kim

He only had one daughter, and she wasn't married.

Ron

So the king set out looking fer a husband for her. He got plenty young fellows

Kim

and a few ol' 'uns.

Tommy

"Li:ł detdunadi, don wodemłanahna: ts'ana, hon do:sho: doyenapkowa kwa' don idonapshukwa da: miwe' kwa' dem alana'man'ona, ełładap hon demł'ona a:wosheman yashenna. Don shokyapdu dem miyashe:nak'yap lehap do'n ho' a:wantse'manna, don emma idona:wa."

Ron & Tommy

Akkya i:yelekk'yanapkya.

Kim

Che'k'wat a:nankwin hish dikwahna'kya.

Ron

Lesnapde, don a:wan'ayyu'ya:naba A:shiw' a:wan wowe, isnhoł kwa' i:wihanukwana:wammen kwa'hoł lesna' dens hanłinapkya. Ma' den'at a:wan haydoshnanne.

Kim

Luk ulohnan'ande imat istk'on Ley deya'kya, la:ł hish kwa'hoł demła illi'kya, elt hołli, ma' che'k'wat kwa'hoł emma illi'kya.

Ron

Lesnapde, yam hish kwa'hoł andesheman'ona tse'mekkya, nana ts'ana andeshemakya. Chuwhoł yam ulohnan ukdun'ona.

Kim

Dobinde e'le' illi'kya, la:ł kwa' oyemshi il'amme'kya.

Ron

Akkya Ley yam e'le' an oyemshi deya'dun'ona deshukkyan a:kya. Hish emma a:tsawak an'habokya

Kim

da: ko:wi'ona hoł a:łashshik'i.

Ron

But none of them suited the king. He'd sent his girl to the best schools.

Kim

She had music training and dance lessons

Ron

and she could speak ever' language in the world.

Kim

And this girl shore didn't want no feller her daddy would pick.

Ron

Them fellers kept coming, she kept turning 'em down, and finally the king got aggravated. He sent out a notice all over the country: *(as King)* "Anybody who wants to marry the king's daughter has got to be able to speak a language she can't speak." And if they couldn't, they was gonna get their heads chopped off.

Kim

That slowed them fellers down some.

Ron

But some still showed up.

Tommy *(as Feller)*
"Parlez-vous Français?"

Kim *(as Princess)*
"Oui, je parle Français."

Ron *(as King)*
"Off with his head."

Ron

Lesnapde Ley an dekkwin kwa' kwa'dikhoł i:de'ch'amme'kya. Ley yam e'le' ts'ina:wo'anna'kowa, hish a:k'okshi'kowa, isnok'on allukk'ekkya.

Kim

An e'le' dene: dap oda: anikk'yapkya

Ron

da: hish ulohnan demła kwa'hoł bena elana'kowa beyep anikwa'kya.

Kim

Luk okya da:chi kwa' chuw ottsi an datchu akshihan'ona andeshemanamkya.

Ron

Uhsona a:tsawak ambikwe:n'amme habełkya, okya kwa' a:wansewahnamkya da: akkya yalukwin Ley ibisadikya. Ley benan kwayk'yakkya lahn'hoł lukky ulohn'an demła łuwala: botdi'kowa. *(Ley yashna)* "Chuwhoł ley an e'l'ona yillun'iyahnan i:n'adin'amme' kwa'hoł bena: kwa hom e'le anik'wam'ona anikwak'yanna." Da: kwa anik'wammap, wi'l' oshokkwihnak'yanna.

Kim

Le'na' de'on akkya a:tsawak ko:wi' yu'lahkudikya.

Ron

Lesnapde dem da: a:de'chiłkya.

Tommy *(Tsawak yashna)*
"Parlez-vous Français?"

Kim *(an E'le' yashna)*
"Oui, je parle Français."

Ron *(Ley yashna)*
"Oshokkwihna:we."

Arden *(as Feller)*
"Como se llama, mama?"

Kim
"Mi nobre es María."

Ron & Tommy
"Off with his head."

Edward *(as Feller)*
"Dom ho' yillun'iyha."
("I want to marry you.")

Kim
"Ma' U."
("It's up to 'U'" [Slang—Zunglish])

Ron, Tommy, & Arden
"Off with his head!"

Ron
The king was having a high ol' time, but he made the mistake of chopping off the head of a witch's son.

Kim
And that ol' witch made a vow she was gonna get even. Before long, strange things started happening to the king and his daughter.

Ron
A pack of wild Zuni dogs moved into the king's basement, and by night they'd travel out over the village terrorizing the people. And anybody who went into the basement got eat up.

Arden *(Tsawak yashna)*
"Como se llama, mama?"

Kim
"Mi nombre es María."

Ron & Tommy
"Oshokkwihna:we."

Edward *(Tsawak yashna)*
"Dom ho' yillun'iyha."

Kim
"Ma' U."

Ron, Tommy, & Arden
"Oshokkwihna:we!"

Ron
Ley an hish ihałuhkya, lesnapde dek'yayała:kya, hałikkw an tsawak'ona' wil' oshokkwihkya.

Kim
Da:chi akkya luk hałik okyattsik yam yasudun'ona beykya. Kwa' dem dela:nammen, Ley dap an e'l'ona a:chiya' ko'alleyapkya.

Ron
Shiwina'kowa wattsida a:wiyosedikowa' Ley an delitdon bal'an isk'on ik'yakweniknan, ko'n dehłi: ukkwe:nan łuwala'kowa a:ho' a:deshlakk'yan a:wallukkya. Da: chowhoł manikkya delitdokwin kwadop, a:widona'kya.

Kim

Then one morning the princess woke up and she was covered in warts from head to toe.

Tommy

Nobody could stand to look at her, much less want to marry her!

Ron

Rats and mice took over the king's kitchen. Thousands of 'em in the food, pots, pans, swimming in the buttermilk. Yech!

Tommy

Meanwhile, Jack lived so far back in the hills, he'd just now got the news about the princess looking fer a husband.

Ron

He thought maybe he'd give his luck a try, so he went to his animal friends and told 'em,

Tommy (as Jack)

"I'm goin' off fer a while. You all look out fer each other while I'm gone."

Arden (as Animal Friend)

"Jack, you better take some of us with you."

Edward (another Animal Friend)

"You know you ain't been no where before."

Dinanda (a third Animal Friend)

"You liable to need a little help."

Kim

Lesna' dobin yadon shamledip, Ley an e'le (princess) okwip, hish demła oshokkwikwin kwayna' dupni:kwin de'china' dakkyana'kya.

Tommy

Kwa' chuw'hoł yayyu'anikdo' un'amme'kya, kop leya' chuhoł yillun'iyhanna!

Ron

Ley an's idoynakya delitdon'ans uhsonas k'ochi dap ts'oklik'o a:wan yokya. Ko:hoł mi:ł de'chi a:wan kwa'hołanna'kowas ukkwadełkya—ido:wa'kowa, dewanna'kowa, saw'anna'kowa, kwik'ya:w'an ichuk'yaye:napkya. Ussa!

Tommy

Da:chi Jack, lukk'on lakhoł le'de yala:w'an k'yakwe'kya, yalu'deyande chim benan ahkya, princess łashshik deshuyn'ona.

Ron

Ma' a:ma honk'wat halo:willik'yanna le'n tse'man akkya yam wema: a:kuwaye dinakwin a:nan le'na' yadinekkya,

Tommy (Jack yashna)

"Wan ho' ko:wi' hoł a:nuwa. Kwa' wan ho' im'ammap, don iyyayyubachipdu."

Arden (Wowe' A:wan Kuwaye yashna)

"Jack, do' i:n'adin'amme ko:hoł'ona ho'na' do' a:willi' a:nuwa."

Edward (doba Wowe' A:wan Kuwaye yashna)

"Do' ayyu'ya:na kwa' kya:k'i' do' hoł a:na'ma."

Dinanda (ha'ik'yanna:na Wowe' A:wan Kuwaye yashna)

"Do' ko'le'ap ko:wi' dapde i:satdo: andeshem'anna."

Tommy
"No, now, I reckon you all better stay here. You know how the people that live in town are. They might not understand us traveling together."

Kim
But now the animals decided that somebody needed to go, and as Jack was leaving, two fleas jumped off his ol' dog onto his coat.

Ron
Jack traveled along

Kim
and traveled along.

Ron
Then he heard,

Kim (*as Cat*)
"Meow, help."

Dinanda (*another Cat*)
"Meow, help."

Tommy
Jack run over to a pond and saw a sack in the water, and the cries was coming from that sack.

Kim & Dinanda
"Meow, help. Meow, help."

Tommy
Jack jerked that sack out of the water and two little kittens fell out.

Tommy
"Holo, wan anak'yat chi ele don demł'ona dinaye. Don ayyu'ya:naba łuwal'an a:ho'i' a:de'ona ko'hoł a:win'ona. Hon i:willaba' a:wallup ko'hoł leya' i:tse'manna, kwa yu'he:dunapshukwa."

Kim
Lesnapde chuhoł akshi' a:dun'ona lukkya wema ts'ana:s i:yelekk'yanapkya, akkya hi:ninishi' hoł Jack a:nap, an wattsit'annan kwili biłasho a:chi la'hina bani:k'yanan an le:w'annan ibatchukya.

Ron
Jack yams hoł haydokwin a:kya

Kim
akkya lesna's a:kya.

Ron
Dekkwande kwa'hoł hadiya:kya,

Kim (*Mu:sa yashna*)
"Maw, hom ansatduna:we."

Dinanda (*doba Mu:sa yashna*)
"Maw, hom ansatduna:we."

Tommy
Jack k'yanakwin ałdikwin ye:lahna yadok'yanan wahdan k'yay'on una'kya, la:ł uhsona wahdan'an k'ona:kwaylekkya.

Kim & Dinanda
"Maw, hom ansatduna:we. Maw, hom ansatduna:we."

Tommy
Jack k'yan'an wahdan łukwe'adina kwayk'yap, kwili mu:sa ts'ana' a:chi biyah kwaykya.

Kim & Dinanda

Nearly drowned and spittin' water. "Psst, phee . . ."

Tommy

"You fellers okay?"

Kim

"Meow, yes, Jack, we're okay now, thanks to you."

Dinanda

"But we're awful cold and hungry."

Tommy

"Well I better just take you with me then."

Ron

So Jack stuck 'em in his coat pockets, so they could warm up, and off he went.

Kim

Next day, Jack come up on some boys playing in the road.

Ron

They had a string tied around a toad frog's leg and ever time he'd jump, they'd jerk him back.

Edward (as Frog)

"Ribet, oh me, oh my. Ribet, oh me, oh my."

Tommy

"Here you all stop that 'fore I snatch you bald-headed."

Kim

Them boys took off running hard as they could go—not 'cause Jack threatened 'em, but because he had done it in frog language.

Kim & Dinanda

Ełt a:chi wakkwadokya'en doms a:chi k'yabuhu'ak'yekkya. "Oh, oh . . ."

Tommy

"Donsh ele'shi?"

Kim

"Maw, e:ye Jack hon ele ke:si, dom tse'makwinn akkya, elahkwa."

Dinanda

"Lesnapde hon ashe: its'umanan da: oshe'a."

Tommy

"Ma' anak'yat doms do'na' ho' illi' a:nuwa."

Ron

Akkyas Jack yam lewan'an wahda'kowas a:chiya' utchu:kya, a:chi yusudidun'ona akkya. Da:s Jack la:ł a:kya.

Kim

Dewap, ko:hoł'ona tsam ts'ana on'an ik'oshe:na:w'an Jack de'chikya.

Ron

Luk a:tsana dakkya an sakwin'an bi'le' anahk'yanapkya, akkya ko'na' i:bu'la'hip, ik'wałt wibi'adina:wa.

Edward (Dakkya yashna)

"Wibit, ya'anna ho:'o. Wibit, ya'anna ho:'o."

Tommy

"Dechun'a ke:si da:ch'at ho' do'na' a:łukwe'adip, don mo'shikdo: yo'anna."

Kim

Uhsona' a:ts'anas hish yam ko'na a:ław'ona yudula'kya—kwa' hish da: Jack ko'hoł a:wallewunam'on akkya, chi leha'ba lesna dakkya an bena:w akkya ben'on akkya yudula'kya.

Tommy

Which is a scary sounding thing to non-frogs.

Edward

"Ribet, oh me, oh my. Ribet, you actually speak toad."

Tommy

"Yes sir I do, and I'm mighty sorry 'bout them human animals. Young 'uns can be mean. Are you all right?"

Edward

"Oh me, oh my, yes I'm fine. My leg's a mite pulled, but I'll be okay."

Tommy

"Well maybe you better come with me. Them boys liable to come back."

Kim

So Jack stuck the toad-frog in his pouch and on he went.

Ron

It was just getting 'bout dark when Jack got up to the palace.

Tommy

Ever' door in town was locked.

Kim

Ever' window barred.

Ron

In a few hours, them dogs would be roaming the streets.

Tommy

Ma' uhsona bena: dophoł atdanni kwa' chuwa dakkya de'ammapba.

Edward

"Wibit, ya'anna ho:'o. Wibit, do' den elleya dokkya'ma beye:'a."

Tommy

"E:ye ma' denna, da:chi ist dom ko'alleyadikya dekkwin hish ho' dom anko'hadi, uhs a:ho'i' wow'annan hi:nina. Uhs a:ts'an'ona ishoł hish a:samu. Domsh ele'shi?"

Edward

"Ya'ana ho:o, ya'ana ho:o, eye hom kwa' ko'ley'amme. Ho' ko:wi' sakwi: hashin'apde, ma' che'k'wat ho' elek'yanna."

Tommy

"Ma' ko'ma honk'wat hom do' il a:nuwa. Uhsi tsats'ana: honk'wat ko'le'ap ik'walt a:wiyanna."

Kim

Akkya isk'ons Jack yam k'wapbon'an dakkya ulunan da:s lał a:kya.

Ron

Hish chim dek'widin lesde:na' Jack Ley an k'yakwe dehyakwin de'chikya.

Tommy

Łuwal'an hoł et'ch'amme' awe:na: an'ułdopkya.

Kim

Demł ashsho'wa: he:doma: a:yałapkya.

Ron

Domt ko:wi' dela:'ap, uhsona wattsida ona'kowa a:wallunna.

Tommy

Jack could hear 'em howlin.

Arden, Edward, & Dinanda (*as Dogs*)

"Ar rowl, ar rowl. Cursed! Cursed!"

Tommy

Jack started thumping on the castle door, "Hey, let me in!"

Ron (*as King*)

"Go away 'fore these dogs eat you."

Tommy

"Let me in. I've come to marry the princess."

Kim

The door flung open and there was the king.

Ron

"Are you crazy? There's mad dogs eatin' people and you're talking 'bout marryin'? Uh, by the way, have you seen the princess lately?"

Tommy

"No I ain't never seed her. But, if I can stop them dogs, can I git a look?"

Ron

"A hundred has tried and a hundred has died, but if you can stop 'em I reckon I might consider you fer a son-in-law."

Kim

Meanwhile them Zuni dogs was carryin' on.

Tommy

Jack yanhadiya:kya, doms k'ona:w ik'eyadopkya.

Arden, Edward, & Dinanda (*Wattsida yashna*)
(*Wohwok'yan*) "An'ashena'kya! An'ashena'kya!"

Tommy

Jack Ley an k'yakwe łan'ans awe:n'ans dopdok'ekkya, "Awshu, hom kwadok'yana:we!"

Ron (*Ley yashna*)

"Łu' le'em holi da:ch'at dom luk wattsida idona:wa."

Tommy

"Hom kwadok'yana:we. Ho' princess'ya yillukyan'iya."

Kim

Awe:nan yetch'amme hoł yałdihap, Ley ela'kya.

Ron

"Dosh wi'winaye? Wattsida a:samu' a:ho'i' a:widona:wap chi do' a:wiyillu: beye:a? A:h, awshu, kwash dem do' princess'ya' lotdemana' un'amme?"

Tommy

"Ełła kwa' dem kya:k'i' ho' un'amme. Anak'yat, honk'wat ist ho' wattsida dechunek'yap, kwa'sh hom do' una:k'yashshukwa?"

Ron

"Asi: asdemł'ona i:de'chunapkya, la:ł asi: asdemł'ona yashekya. Ma' do' dechunek'yap ma' honk'wat hom do' da:lak yodun'ona ho' tse'manna."

Kim

Ła:ł da:chi dem hish A:shiw a:wan wattsida kwa' ihałuhk'yana:wamme'kya.

Arden, Edward, & Dinanda
"Ar rowl, ar rowl. Cursed! Cursed!"

Tommy
"Give me some food and a light and shut the door behind me."

Ron
"No time fer that! So long Jack." *(King shoves Jack into the basement.)*

Kim
Jack started easing his way down into that dark basement.

Arden, Edward, & Dinanda
"Ar rowl, ar rowl."

Tommy
"Hey fellers it's me, Jack!"

Kim
Them dogs couldn't believe Jack could talk their language.

(Arden, Edward, and Dinanda begin to carry on in Zuni. Jack listens, shaking his head, like he understands.)

Tommy
"Now let me get this straight. The witch buried a human skull in the basement. You all have to stay here and guard it and eat nothin' but humans 'til somebody digs up the skull. Is 'at 'bout it?"

Arden, Edward, & Dinanda
"You got it, Jack!"

Arden, Edward, & Dinanda
(Wohwok'yan) "An'ashena'kya! An'ashena'kya!"

Tommy
"Hom ido: dap habiyan a:wukna:we, lesnan ho' kwadokya dap awe:nan aɫduna:we."

Ron
"Kwa' la:ɫ dela:shukwa! Ma's ɫu:'u, Jack." *(Ley Jack'ya' k'yakwe manikkyakwin uladena kwadok'ekkya.)*

Kim
Jack yu'ɫahkuna's manikkya delitdon dek'win ulikwin bani:kya.

Arden, Edward, & Dinanda
(Wohwo'anna)

Tommy
"She:... a:kuwaye, ho:'o, ho' Jack!"

Kim
A:wan bena:w akkya Jack a:washhu'wapba uhsona wattsida kwa hish iɫdemana:wamme'kya.

(Arden, Edward, dap Dinanda shiwi'ma dey'unapkya. Jack yu'hadiya:k'yakkya, lesnan yam oshokwinn akkya sewahk'yakkya, yu'hedun ikna.)

Tommy
"Ma' a:ma wan hish ho' benan aɫmoɫa:du. Halik okyattsik hap'an dom'oshokkwin manikkya i:delit'an balo:kya. Akkya don demɫ'ona liɫ ayyubatchi' dinaye, da: akkya doms don a:ho'i' idoyna:we, dem kya:k'i' chuhoɫ haba dom'oshokkwin balohdundekkwi. Lesn hoɫi'shi?"

Arden, Edward, & Dinanda
"Do' ahkya, Jack!"

Ron

So Jack dug up the skull and let them dogs out of the basement. They're still running around all over the village, never did go home.

Kim

The king was overjoyed.

Ron

"Jack you done it! I can't believe it! I had dog experts from all over the world, but none of 'em had ever seen nothin' like them Zuni dogs."

Tommy

"Well thank you King, but I've sorty worked up an appetite. Reckon I could get some supper?"

Ron

"Uh, well Jack, you see, uh, well, uh since we've had this dog problem, I've lost my kitchen help and we been eating Chu Chu's pizza a lot lately. But, uh, you go on to the kitchen and if you can find anything you're welcome to it. I'd go with you but uh, I better go check on the princess, tell her the good news."

Kim

Jack went on to the kitchen, but when he tried to open the door, them rats and mice was so thick the door would barely move.

Tommy

When Jack finally squeezed in,

Kim

that door slammed shut.

Ron

Akkyas Jack haba dom'oshokkwin balohnan wattsida manikkya i:delit'an upbo'kowa ukkwe:k'yakkya. Ma' dem akkya la:k łuwalan demła a:wallu, kwa' kya:k'i' yam k'yakwekwin a:wa:namkya.

Kim

Ley hish bushkwe:na' k'ettsadikya.

Ron

"Jack do' lesde lewukya! Kwa' ho' hish iłdemana'ma! Ulohnan demła wattsida akkya a:wanik'ona hom illap a:deya'kya, lesnapde kwa' chowandik hoł kya:k'i kwa'hoł Shiw' an wattsida ikna' a:wuna:wamme'kya."

Tommy

"Ma' elahkwa Ley, lesnapde hish ho' oshemadikya. Anak'yat kwa'sh hom idok'yana'shukwa?"

Ron

"A:h, ma' Jack, do' dun'ap, a:h, ma', a:h ko'na' wattsida akkya idenidikya dap, hom an ido:washe:napkowa dehwa:napkya, akkya wans hish hon Chu Chu an pizza akkya a:wa:kya. Lesnapde, ma', la:ł ido:washe:nak'yannankwin bikwayi. Honk'wat do' kwa'hoł awap, ma' do' yam ko'na' tse'man'ona' de'udu."

Kim

Jack ido:washe:nak'yannankwin bikwe:nan, awe:nan ałdihan'iyhap, istk'on k'ochi dap ts'okłik hish emma dey'on akkya awe:nan ko'napde yałdihkya.

Tommy

Ko'napde hoł Jack iłatts'una bikwe:k'yap,

Kim

uhsona awe:nan hish ława'adina yałdi'kya.

Tommy

And Jack was standing in rats up to his knees.

Kim

And they was all staring at him

Tommy

licking their jaws.

Ron

'Bout that time them two kittens poked their heads out. They smelled supper.

Kim & Dinanda *(as Cats)*

"Looks like you could use some help Jack."

Ron

Jack never seed nothing like it. Didn't take 'em half an hour to clean out them rodents. Then them kittens stretched out on the hearth, went sound asleep.

Tommy

Jack figgered he wadn't as hungry as he thought. He figgered he'd maybe order one of them pizzas later, went lookin' fer the princess.

Kim

The princess was not about to show herself, warts and all, to nobody.

Ron

The king was on his way down stairs when Jack found him.

Tommy

"How long did you say you'd been eatin' pizzas? That kitchen could use some cleaning."

Tommy

Jack elaye, oshshikwin de'china' k'ochi an'habonaye.

Kim

La:ł demł'ona hish domt anmosanana: a:deya'kya

Tommy

doms łewechi: its'upłinapkya.

Ron

Leshoł a:na' mu:s a:chiya' oshokkwi: ichuk'oskukya. A:chi kwa'hoł idona'dun'ona dechi:wanahkya.

Kim & Dinanda *(a:chi Musa yashna)*

"Holon do' i:satdo: andeshem'anna Jack."

Ron

Kwa' kya:k'i' le'na' kwa'hoł Jack dun'amme'kya. Hish domt le:' dela:'ap a:chi uhsona' k'ochi denk'yakkya. Isk'ons mu:s a:chi aklikyan'an its'ałinans ashe: ałkya.

Tommy

Isk'on Jack an dophoł tsemakwi: deya'kya. Kwa's oshemanamkya. Domt tse'manan hinik ana dela:'ap dens domt pizza shemanna. Princess'ya' deshukkyan a:kya.

Kim

Da:chi princess kwa' chuwhoł an iyu'he:dokk'yana'-man'iyahkya, yam dakkyan'ona dap kwa'hoł demła ko'hoł in'ona akkya.

Ron

Ley łewe' i:yetchi'kowa bani:kyan a:nap, lehap Jack awakya.

Tommy

"Hay ko:wi'p delana:na' don pizza idona' a:deyaye? Uhsi ido:washnakya delitdon'an yuladohna'dun'ona' lesde:na."

Ron

"I know Jack. I'm sorry. I just hoped—you got rid of them dogs, and I thought . . . maybe—but I guess it was too much to . . ."

Tommy

"Oh them rats is gone."

Ron

"Gone! I don't believe it! Jack you are a man atter my heart."

Tommy

"It ain't your heart I come atter. I'd shore like to meet the princess."

Ron

"Uh, well Jack maybe we better wait 'til morning. She don't exactly look her best right now."

Kim

The next day, the princess sneaked a peek at Jack waiting downstairs and realized this was no ordinary feller, and that the only way he was gonna leave was to let him look at her.

Ron

Jack had been having a conversation with his friend the frog, who spotted the princess first.

Edward (as Frog)

"Ribet, lordy Jack, she's beautiful! Look!"

Tommy

"Where? Gulp."

Ron

"Ho' ayyu'ya:na Jack. Aw'iyo do:'o. Ho' domt ants'ummehkya—do' honk'wat wattsida dechunek'yakkya dap da: la:ł ho' tse'map . . . domt hish honk'wadi:w akkya—lesnapde hish da honk'wat emma deya'kya . . ."

Tommy

"Awshu uhsona k'ochi kwa's dechuwwa."

Ron

"Kwa' dechuwwa! Kwa' ho' iłdemana'ma! Jack hish hom' an ik'e:nan do' andeshem'an'ona."

Tommy

"Kwa' dom' an ik'e:nan ho' andeshemana'ma, kwa' uhsona akkya ho' inamkya. Hish ho' hiyo:lishna' princess'ya' unak'yan'iyha."

Ron

"A:h, ma' wan a:ma dewan shamle chimi Jack. Le:wi' a:na' kwa' hish da: yam ko'n ho'i' koksh'ona' dey'amme."

Kim

Dewap shamle, princess de'ona ik'olo' dunabikway:nan Jack manikya shoky'ap una'kya. Luk tsawak kwa' dens hish dekkwande chuwhoł de'amme'kya, da: i:nadin'amme princess'ya unak'yan'iyahkya, da:ch'at kwa' dehwa:shukwa.

Ron

Jack yam kuwaye, dakkya, ashshu'wende uhsona dakkya princess'ya kela ank'ohak'yakkya.

Edward (Dakkya yashna)

"Wibit, Jack, hish e'k'okshi! Una!"

Tommy

"Hopbi?" (Hish k'yap ikwilikya.)

Kim

The princess could see the look on his face, "So, you want to marry me? Well Jack, come and seal it with a kiss!"

Tommy

Jack was not one to back down, but there was no way he could kiss this frog-woman. Frogs was fine. Women, fine. But a frog-woman—never!

Ron

By now the frog was in heaven.

Edward

"Look at that. Oh my goodness! Jack get up close to her."

Kim

The princess heard the frog carryin' on and thought Jack was making fun of her, so she walked right up to him and stuck her lips out, "Go on dog-boy, kiss me if you dare!"

Ron

That frog saw his chance. "Smack, slurp!" Right on the lips, that tongue flying ever' which way over them warts.

Kim

"Oh, my goodness!"

Kim

Jack hish nobon ko'inadip, princess una'kya, "Awo homsh do' yillun'iyha'shi? Ma' ko'ma, Jack k'yałem' a:nan hom ts'upłi akkya dom benan hashinak'yanna!"

Tommy

Jack kwa' kwa'hoł akkya k'ełukk'e:n'am'ona, lesnapde dishshomahha kwa' ko'lehoł luk dakky-okya' dey'ona ts'upłishukwa. Dakkya de'chi dap kwa' ko'ley'amme. Okya' dap kwa' ko'le'amme. Lesnapde dakky' dap okya' imden'ap—ya'usa!

Ron

Dachi dakkya hish hoł imo'kya, hish an ihałuhkya.

Edward

"Lakkwash una. O:...elu, Jack allotdek'ya."

Kim

Dakkya kwa's hish delokk'yadik'yana'map, princess an'hadiya:nan tse'map Jack ko'anikwe:'a le'hadinan Jack'ya' inkwin a:nan yam ishhi: yo'do:kya, "Hana'de wattsida-tsawak'i, hom ts'upłi wenan dosh yayyu'anikt'doye!"

Ron

Uhsona' dakkya yam dehwan una'kya. "Tsupłikya!" Ishshi:wa'kowa. Doms an honnin le'ep la'chokkya, an dakkyana'kowa.

Kim

"O:...elu!"

Tommy

And there, before Jack, stood the most beautiful woman he'd ever seen. Skin the color of sunlight, hair red as a cardinal's wing and thick as a horse's mane, falling from her head to the floor. Jack was in love!

Kim

But the princess had seen the look in Jack's eye when she was ugly, and she decided to test him. "Men never look at real beauty. They look at the surface. Tell me Jack, what color is my hair?"

Tommy

"Ree—"

Kim

"Wait! I'm gonna give you a fair chance. You have 'til tomorrow. If you can tell me the color of my hair, maybe I'll consider you fer a husband."

Ron

Now, while all this was going on, them two little fleas that Jack had brought from home was fallin' in love, just like Jack and the frog, but it was the princess' hair that they was in love with.

Dinanda *(as Flea)*

"Oh my goodness, if I could just run up and down from the top of her head to her toes in that hair."

Tommy

La:ł isk'ons, Jack el'ande, hish chuwa e'k'okshi' ela'kya. Kwa' kya:k'i' le'na' chuwhoł un'amme'kya. Hish ho'i' yadokkya an dek'ohannan ikna' lomomon deyan, hish ts'aba shilowa an ebissen ikna daya: shilowa'kya da: hish du:sh an tsipbokyałan ikna' daya yahoni'kya, oshokkwikwin kwayna' awełakwin de'china' an daya: dashana'kya. Jack hish hiyo:łishna' hannilikya!

Kim

Lesnapde da:chi princess ayyu'ya:na'kya, dem hish princess ayyats'ap, Jack ko'hoł leya' una'kowa' akkya da:chi attsu'man'iyahkya. "Den'ats a:wottsi' kwa' hish da: chuwhoł hiyo:łishna' dewłash ho'ona unapshukwa. Domt hish chowaya' yałdo yalun una:wa. Hom adine Jack, ko'p hom daya: a:wina?"

Tommy

"A:shi—"

Kim

"Wanni! Do' tse'matdun'ona akkya dom ho' dehwan uts'i. Wan dem dewani. Wenan ho' ko'hoł daya: in'ona' do' an'awap, ma' honk'wat do' hom łashhik yodun'ona ho' tse'manna."

Ron

Ke:si, le'hol leyabap, da:chi luk kwili biłasho a:chi, Jack an k'yak'wan a:chi aksh iykowa, uhsona a:chi hish hanilidikya. Ko'n Jack a:chi dakkyakwin lewukowa. Lesnapde lukk'on a:chi hish princess an daya:w akkya ko'kwayuchidikya.

Dinanda *(Biłasho yashna)*

"O:...elu, e:t hish ho' domt an daya:w' an ye:lahna baniyun'iyha, oshokk'wan kwayna' an dupni:kwin de'china."

Arden (*as second Flea*)
"I could just die happy. I could just die happy."

Ron
So in that hair they jumped. All night Jack tried his best to figger out what the princess had meant.

Tommy
"Tell me the color of my hair? Dang it, it's red! Red as a cardinal's wing!"

Kim
But Jack knowed it was a trick question and he was afraid he was gonna fail.

Ron
Meanwhile, the fleas was in hair heaven, and they discovered the secret.

Kim
There, hidden deep in the center of her head was one single strand of snow white hair, covered by thousands and thousands of bright red strands. The princess knew, but her vanity had never before let her tell.

Ron
The next morning she combed out her hair and left it loose flowing to the floor.

Kim
"What color is my hair, Jack?"

Ron
Each of the fleas jumped into one of Jack's ears.

Arden (*Kwilik'yanna:na Bilasho yashna*)
"Ma' lesna' dap ho' k'ettsan ashenna. Ma' lesna' dap ho' k'ettsan ashenna."

Ron
Akkyas uhsona daya:w' an a:chi i:bu'la'hikya. Dehlinan denna Jack hish princess an benan ko'hoł ikwekkowa ayyu'he:den i:nekkya.

Tommy
"A:ma hom adine ko'p ho' daya: ina? Ma' imat a:shilowa! Ts'apba shilow a' an ebissen ikna' a:shilowa!"

Kim
Jack ayyaładinak'yap, ayyu'ya:na'kya che'k'wat domt ani:de'chiban'ona. Jack tse'map honk'wat kwa' ele de'ushukwa le'hadikya.

Ron
Da:chi lesi' a:na' princess an oshokk'wan bilasho a:chiya' hish daya:w' an ihaluhkya, isk'on hoł a:chi kwa'hoł ik'olo'kowa awakya.

Kim
Lakhoł hish princess an oshokk'wan idiwa dobinde dayan k'ohanna akshi'kya, ko:hoł mił de'chi' hish daya: a:shilowa akkya bo'ya'kya. Princess e:t ayyu'ya:na'kya, lesnapde i:wichem'an'on akkya kwa' kya:k'i' benamkya.

Ron
Dewap shamle hish eledokna' ibishnan yam daya: awełakwin a:bani:k'ekkya.

Kim
"Ko'p ho' daya: ina, Jack?"

Ron
Bilasho a:chi i:bu'la'hinan a:chi Jack an lashhokdi:wa'kowa' a:chi isamma: kwadokya.

Arden & Dinanda *(as Fleas)*
"Red!"
"White!"

Tommy
"What?"

Arden & Dinanda
"Red!"
"White!"

Tommy
"You all are crazy!"

Arden & Dinanda
"Red!"
"White!"

Tommy
"Red and white?!"

Kim
The princess couldn't believe it! No one had ever looked at her that close before. "Jack, I reckon I might consider you fer a husband."

Tommy
On the day of the wedding, two doves flew down and lit on Jack and the princess' shoulders

Kim
and whispered the words of the ceremony to them in the language of love.

Ron
Atter they was married

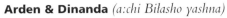

Arden & Dinanda *(a:chi Bilasho yashna)*
"Shilowa!"
"K'ohanna!"

Tommy
"Kwa'bi?"

Arden & Dinanda
"Shilowa!"
"K'ohanna!"

Tommy
"Don demł'ona a:wi'winaye!"

Arden & Dinanda
"Shilowa!"
"K'ohanna!"

Tommy
"Shilowa' dap k'ohanna?!"

Kim
Kwa' princess hish ildemanamkya! Kwa' kya:k'i' chuwhoł lesna' ele lotde un'amme'kya. "Jack, ma' imat hom do' lashshik deya'dun'ona ho's tse'manna."

Tommy
Achi i:wiyillunnande, uhsona yadon'an kwili ni:sha:bak k'ohan a:chi la'hina bani:k'yanan Jack dap princess a:chi an chut'an immiyałdo:nan

Kim
hish delokk'yana' a:chi i:wichemanakya bena:w akkya, Jack a:chiya' Princess-kwin i:wiyyillukya.

Ron
A:chi i:wiyyillukya'en

Kim

they spent part of the time in the castle

Ron

and part of their time in the mountains

Kim

where the princess learned to talk to all the animals.

Ron

Now this story just goes to show you . . .

Kim

you don't have to be rich to be smart.

Tommy

You don't even have to be smart to be rich.

Kim

And the most important language of all

All

is the language of the heart.

(Harvest dancers enter and stand upstage.)

Kim

a:chi ishoł castle an imon

Ron

da: ishoł a:chi yala:wa'kowa dek'ekkya

Kim

isk'on princess kwa'hoł wema: dap wowe' a:washshu'we: yanikwadikya.

Ron

Akkya lukkya' benan do'n a:wan yu'he:dokk'ekkya . . .

Kim

kwa' hish da: do' li:ku:w akkya kwa'hoł anikwa'shukwa.

Tommy

Kwa' hish da: domt do' yam anikwa:w akkya li:kundeya'shukwa.

Kim

La:ł luk hish i:n'adin'amme benan dehy'ona

Demł'ona

benan ik'e:n'annan dey'ona.

(Sade'chi: Odi:kwe ukkwadonan, iłuwayaldok'yanna.)

Zuni Fall

A:shiwi A:wan Miyashe:nak'ya

Arden

Now harvest time comes to the people. The crops are gathered—corn, melons, squash, and wheat. All are sent up to the village where the women have prepared special storage rooms.

Edward

Once stored properly, the people of the Middle Place feel fulfilled. The year has been good; therefore the Sun Priest, or another spiritual leader, summons the people.

Arden

He proclaims that the harvest is made. That it is plentiful. That the obligations have been met, and now time will be spent together. Word of the coming harvest dance echoes through the village. Everyone's thoughts are on the dance. Every night, the dancers—boys and girls—meet to practice.

Edward

The big day comes. At dawn, everywhere in the village there is cooking. The grains and herbs grown from the fields are used. Many loaves of bread are baked. Girls help by drawing water, while boys chop wood.

Arden

Miyashe:nakwin a:dey'chinna. Lesna' a:deya:kwin a:wan kwa'hols lena:, kwa'hol do:shonan demłanahna: a:łashanna. Yam heshoda:kwin doshonan demła uwak'yanapkowa a:yemakk'yana:wa. Holnoł do:shonan delitdo:wa'kowa, a:wokya, luknok'on yelekk'yana:wa.

Edward

A:wan mipkosnabap, ma'che'k'wat a:ho' i:k'ettsananna. Luk debikwaynan yele'kon akkya ho' i:k'ettsana. Da:ch a:wan Bekwin holi, chuhoł yam a:ho' a:wil iyan'ona, benan kwayk'yanna.

Arden

E:ye. Miyashe:na'kya, kwa'hoł lena: uwakya. Ho'n a:wan tsemakwi: yele'kyadap, hon iyyayyułashshik'yana:wa, le'na hoł benap, Sade'chi: odan kwaydun'ona benan łuwala'kowa idulohanna. Aho' odi: i:tse'manna. He:...ma' che'k'wat chi ko'n dehłi: habelanna, e:washdok dap a:tsawak'i.

Edward

Haydokwin de'chip, yadokweyip, le:' łuwalan hoł etch'amme' ido:wo'anna, yam kwa'hoł lena:napkowa uhsi'de akkya. Mulobap, e:washdok k'yawishna:wap :ch a:tsawak łebakchona:wa.

Arden

Meanwhile, all the dancers from the village start fitting themselves into their ceremonial costumes. In their regalia, the dancers, including the singers, gather outside the big plaza, soon to be packed with onlookers. Once everyone is in place, the singing starts and the harvest dancers enter. Dancing continues until about noon, when the food that was prepared is brought forth. The religious leaders are the first to take morsels to honor Mother Earth and also to honor the ancestors in order that they, too, can join the day. Soon the whole village is eating until all are satisfied.

Edward

Guests from other tribes and communities are present. Good feelings and words are shared. Some barter seeds until, again, the Harvest Dance comes. Now there is nothing but color in the plaza. Girls, boys, and singers are dressed beautifully, "Hish chikwannaye."

Dinanda

The girls—some are bare around the shoulders and legs, while others are in full costume. Their feet are covered with white buckskin moccasins and leggings. The rest of their body is covered with a black manta, worn over one shoulder. A red sash and a white sash are tied around the manta at the waist. A white cape with black and red stripes is worn around the back of the shoulders.

Edward

A full necklace of turquoise, coral, and strings of shell, along with a squash blossom necklace, boasts the chest. The headwear is a combination of colorful braids, a squash blossom, ornamented board, and many plumes of parrot and eagle. These girls move gracefully with a special kind of beauty, like that of an eagle's fluff—full bodied and delicate.

Arden

Odipdun'ona yam kwa'hoɫ ɫeya: iya:k'yana:wa. Odipdun'ona dap denena:kwes a:ya:na dehwitdo ɫan' an habelanna. A:ho'i, demaya:kwe, domt ko:wi dela:ap habonna. Isk'on dena: kwayyip, sade'chi odi:kwe's ukkwadonna. Odiwa:… idiw'aps hoɫ lesde:na ido: yele'kowas habonna. Isk'on kwa'hoɫ akkya le'na ɫuwal'ona dewus akkya a:ho' a:dey'ona, luknok'on kel ido: yele'kowa isnhoɫ dehakchonan yam Awidelin Tsitda, lesdik leya a:wan a:lashhina: aweletchokkowa a:wan haydos a:wik'e:na deliya:na:wa. Isk'on uhsona kwa'hoɫ demɫa yele'kyade'an le:' ɫuwal'ona demɫa ansammo wans yadonilli idonak'yanna.

Edward

Da:chi le:' ɫuwala: kwayna a:ho'i hok'yan hoɫ a:wikowa uhsona idonak'yanna'kowa isnhoɫ iyyashshu'wa, benan k'oksh akkya iyyayaɫashona:wa. Kwa'hoɫ do:shonan i:yadeɫnak'yanna. Lesak'yadip, Sade'chi da:s odi:wa. Ma' les a:na' hish dehwit'an odi:kwe habon'ap hish kwa'hoɫ tso'yannishshi' de'chi. E:washdok'i, a:tsawak'i, da: denena:kwe, demɫ habon'ona dikwahn a:yanaye. Hish chikwannaye.

Dinanda

A:wokya, hamme' chudi: dap oma: a:si'sik'yayaye. Hamme' a:de'ona da:ch hish demɫ a:ya:naye. Dowa mokk'wa dap kew'ikkwi: a:k'ohanna. Ehe:we a:yadonaban e'ni: dap molimmon ikkwi: ts'ulukda:wa'kowa a:wikkwiba. Kutcha k'ohan a:ba'iba.

Edward

La:ɫ ɫi'akwa dap alaho dap k'ohakwa ts'up daku:we, da: mopdaku:we bo'hada'kowa a:dakuba. La:ɫ oshokkwikwin isk'on a:tso'ya' a:ya:naye—chido: dap, adeya:we dap, lem hakdowe. Laɫ emma mula lawe' dap k'yak'yali uk'yahaya:we. Luk e:washdok eludeya' yodiba, he:…hish doba'm hoɫ a:we'k'okshi. Hish k'yak'yal an u'k'yahayan ikna e'l ihaɫuhn'amme a:dek'yanna.

Dinanda

The boys are in red buckskin moccasins and leggings. The white kachina ceremonial kilts are wrapped around the hips and waist and supported by a red sash and a white and green embroidered sash. Their torsos are bare, their chests partially covered by the necklaces of turquoise, coral, and shell beads. A single eagle fluff adorns each head.

Arden

And the singers are just as colorful!

Edward

Now songs echo throughout the pueblo. As one group enters with a song, another appears at the opposite end, singing loud to out do the first. As the groups draw together, in mild competition, everyone's pulse races.

Arden

The dancing continues all day. Then about the time when the sun falls low, when all the groups have entered the plaza, "ehhe!" (*"Yes!"*), the grand finale, the "big dance" comes.

Dinanda

Now it is not unreal to think that the whole world is singing, because the songs, sung from the top of the lungs, resonate everywhere, even to the distant corn fields. Look, here comes the Harvest Dance.

Dinanda

Lał da:ch a:wottsi' a:dey'ona dowa mokk'wa: dap kekewuła: a:shilowa. Da: kok a:wan biłła: a:wuliba. E'ni: dap Dakun Ikkwi: ts'ulukda'kowa a:wikkwiba. Łuni: a:si'si'k'yayan, bo'hada'kowa' da: le:' apdaku: łana—li'akwa' dap alaho dap k'ohakwa ts'upda:ku:we—lesn a:dakuba. Lał doballela a:lashowaba.

Arden

Dene:na:kwe: dem da: lesna'dik leya' a:tso'ya!

Edward

Ke:si, łuwal'an demł hoł dena: botdiye. Liwan hok'yandikhoł a:de'ona denan akkya a:bikweyip, da: hamme' hok'yan a:bikweyip, che'k'wat iyyayyadonakya akkya ashe: denabanna. Iyannikdohna:wap, hish deyadinna, domt i:k'ettsananna.

Arden

Yadonil odi:we. He:...yadon biyahhan lesde:na' ma's demła dana: ukkwe:lep, ehhe! Isk'ons hish iyyayyadełnak'ya. Hish hiyo:lishna' "odin łana" kwayyi.

Dinanda

Hish ulohnan demła denaban ikna hish domt dena: sała'ana. Lahnhoł deyatchi:wa'kowa' de'china' deha:don k'eyadok'yanna. Ma's ist sade'chi: a:bikwayi.

Harvest Dance

(Slow steady beat. Meant for a large group and to encourage spectators to join in. The lyrics speak of bringing a song—"I will sing a beautiful song for you.")

(Dance concludes. Dancers form a semi-circle upstage.)

(Flute begins, singers pick up the song.)

Ron, Tommy, & Kim
Bright Morning Star *(song)*
Bright morning star's arising
Bright morning star's arising
Bright morning star's arising
Day is a-breakin' in my soul.

Oh where are our dear mothers
Oh where are our dear mothers
Oh where are our dear mothers
Day is a-breakin' in my soul.

Where are our dear fathers
Where are our dear fathers
Where are our dear fathers
Day is a-breakin' in my soul.

They have gone to heaven a-singing
They have gone to heaven a-singing
They have gone to heaven a-singing
Day is a-breakin' in my soul.

Bright morning star's arising
Bright morning star's arising
Bright morning star's arising
Day is a-breakin' in my soul.

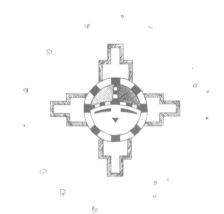

Sade'chi: Odanne

(Yu'lahkuna' domdo'ana. Luk odan em'ona odipdun'ona, akkya demaya:kwe' iwosli'dun'ona' ihakk'yabanna. Denan'an kwa'hoł tso'ya denap'dunona beye:'a—"Do'na' ho' a:wan denan tso'ya ho' dena'unna.")

(Denan chun'ap, odi:kwe idullapna' mas'an iłuwayaldok'ya.)

(Bu:bunan ts'ana' ik'oshna kwayyi, denena:kwe' iwoslik'ya.)

Ron, Tommy, & Kim
Mo' Kwa:n Osena Walolonne *(denanne)*
Mo' Kwa:n Osena walolon ik'eyadok'ya
Mo' Kwa:n Osena walolon ik'eyadok'ya
Mo' Kwa:n Osena walolon ik'eyadok'ya
Hom shełna'an loks yadokwayi.

Awshu hop ho'n a:wan elu a:tsitda
Awshu hop ho'n a:wan elu a:tsitda
Awshu hop ho'n a:wan elu a:tsitda
Hom shełna'an loks yadokwayi.

Awshu hop ho'n a:wan elu a:datchu
Awshu hop ho'n a:wan elu a:datchu
Awshu hop ho'n a:wan elu a:datchu
Hom shełna'an loks yadokwayi.

Yam hoł iyude'chinahnapdundekkwin denena: a:wa:kya
Yam hoł iyude'chinahnapdundekkwin denena: a:wa:kya
Yam hoł iyude'chinahnapdundekkwin denena: a:wa:kya
Hom shełna'an loks yadokwayi.

Mo' Kwa:n Osena walolon ik'eyadok'ya
Mo' Kwa:n Osena walolon ik'eyadok'ya
Mo' Kwa:n Osena walolon ik'eyadok'ya
Hom shełna'an loks yadokwayi.

Zuni Winter
A:shiwi A:wan Dehts'idinna

Edward

Now winter falls on the people. The village slows down. The people tell stories, ancient tales and old histories. When the snow falls, while everything is caped in white and silence is in the air, our Mother Earth rests. Likewise, our children, the Corn Maidens, sleep.

Arden

The people ensure that the seeds get rest. Like a baby, the corn family is rocked, as though in a cradle, and lullabies are sung to them. All rest. The days to come will be for religious observation and fasting, hoping for more blessing.

Edward

People lived like this since the Time of the Beginning, fending for themselves. There was no procrastination. The people supported each other willingly. When it came to planting, the seed family was nurtured by the community, season after season.

Arden

Once a way of life, now this is but a poetic reflection. Today, we do not persevere on behalf of the seed family and Mother Earth. Can this be part of the reason for the illness throughout the land?

Edward

Le'na's łuwal'an dehts'idinna. Łuwal'ans wan yu'łahk'udinna. Benałashi:w dap delapna:w wans uhs'ona' akkya iyyayyułashshik'yannak'yanna. U'łał biyahhap, kwa'hoł k'ohannan bot'ap, delokk'yanan k'eyat'ap, ho'n a:wan Awidelin Tsitda iyude'chinahanna. Lesdik leya, ho'n a:wan chawe, A:dow E:washdok'i, wans ya:delanna.

Arden

Łuwalan demła yam doshonan wans ya:dełk'yana:wa. Wihats'an ikna' wans a:dałna:wa. Yałdon'an alla ikna. Lałs a:wandenabanna. Chuw' etch'amme's iyude'chinahanna. Wans isk'on kwa'hoł dewusu' dewanan akkya a:dek'yanna. Ittsu'manak'yanna.

Edward

Lak'yande'ma ho'n a:wan a:łashshina:w a:deya'kowa le'na i:yanilli a:wiykya. Kwa' yamik'ya: a:dey'amme'kya. Le'na' kwa'hoł yu'anikdo' i:yansatdena' a:wiykya. Le'na yam lena:we, yam kwa'hoł doshonan, antse'mana' lak'yande'ma a:wiykya. Delakwayyi, olo'ik'ya, miyashe:nak'ya, dehts'ina, lesna' a:wiykya.

Arden

Le'n yanil a:deyakyadey'an, la:ks uhsona doms hon i:tse'me:'a. Ma' honk'wat le'na dey'on akkya le:' delana:'ap, kwa' yam do:shonan anshihmakkya, kwa' Awidelin Tsitda anshihmakkya, a:dey'ammon akkya, le'na kwa'hoł weyakkya, ho'n a:wan ulohn'annan botdiye?

Dinanda

We were once a people like this, the Children of the Middle Place.

Solemn Zuni song

(Steady, slow drum beat, constant rattles in the background.)

All

Homeward Now *(song)*

Homeward now, shall I journey,
Homeward upon the rainbow.
Homeward now, shall I journey,
Homeward upon the rainbow.
To life unending and beyond it,
Yea, homeward now shall I journey.
To joy unchanging and beyond it,
Yea, homeward now shall I journey.

(Lights dim, then brighten. Cast bows, thanking the audience.)

Dinanda

Le'n hon a:ho' adeya'kya, Idiwanan An Chawe.

Ayyułashshina' delokk'yana' denak'yanna

(Shiw' an deha:donanna. Doms yułahkuna domdo'anna, mas'an chilili'anna.)

Demł'ona

Yam Heshoda:kwi Ke:si *(denanne)*

Yam heshoda:kwi ke:si, si ho's a:nuwa,
Yam heshoda:kwin amidolanne akkya a:nuwa.
Yam heshoda:kwi ke:si, si ho's a:nuwa,
Yam heshoda:kwin amidolanne akkya a:nuwa.
Hoł dek'ohannan kwa' ibałdok'e:na'mankwi,
E:ha yam heshodakwin ke:si, si ho's a:nuwa.
Hoł isha'małde i:k'ettsanna' a:deyakwi,
E:ha yam heshodakwin ke:si, si ho's a:nuwa.

(Habiyan yu'lahkuna' aklałinna, lesnan ik'wałt ihabiyak'yanna. Delapna:kw idebowak'yanna, demaya:kwe' elahkwa: yaknak'yanna.)

Epilogue

Yalu'dennishshi Benanne

Arden

One time, when I was a young boy, eleven or twelve years old, my grandfather asked me to learn a song he had just composed for a kiva dance. So I sat down by him to learn this new song.

After he had sung the song to me several times, to where I felt comfortable to sing it on my own, he told me I must now carry this new song to the kiva. He said that I must do this for him because he was not feeling well. Then I got really nervous, but my grandfather encouraged me saying that it would be okay and that these men would listen to the new song. Before rising, I sang the song one more time.

I left the house for the kiva which was only about forty yards away. As I walked humming the song, suddenly a dog barked at me. I lost the song. Now I had to turn and go back to ask all over again. My grandfather just laughed and sang it to me.

Again, I left for the kiva humming the song. Now two or three dogs chimed in, and there went the song! My grandfather did not laugh as much this time, but again he gave me the song. Again I set forth, and after several more tries, I made it to the kiva.

I was really nervous when I finally walked in. I greeted the men, "K'n don dewanan a:deyaye?" and sat down. Before they could start singing, I spoke out, saying I had a song from my grandfather. They began teasing me

Arden

Kya:k'yan ho' tsam ts'an'ap, ho' asdemłan dobinde yałdo hombish asdemłan kwili yałdo' debikwayik'yana' dey'ap, hom nana up'e' an denan chim ashkowa ho' yanikwadidun'ona hom ayyała'kya. Akkya ho's ambatchi' i:mup, hom an denekkya.

Ko:wi'hołk'yan hom' an dena'up, ma's ho' samma deyande denep, hom les'anikwekkya, ho' luk denan chim'ona kokko upkwin ley' a:nuwa. Kwa' an tsemakwi: el'ammap akkya an dehw'an ho' a:nuwa, hom le'anikwekkya. Isk'ons ho' deshladikya, lesnapde hom ambuwa'shok'ekkya. Kwa' ko'leya'shukwa, luk a:łashshik habon'ona denan chim'ona an'hadiya:na:wa. Kwa elemaknammen, ho' ałna't dobink'yan dena:kya.

Ho's (ki:wihtsi'kwin) kokko upkwin a:nakya akkya k'yak'wan kwayikya, domt lem dey'an e:t deya'kya. Ho's delokk'yana' yandenen a:nap, dekkwande hom wattsida anwohwodik'yakkya. Ho's denan okk'yakkya. Ho's i:lohk'yanan da:s ik'wałt yała'kyan a:kya. Domt hom nana shikwin, da: ałna't hom' an dena:kya.

Ałna't da:s kokko upkwin ho' yandenen a:kya. Les a:na' kwili, hombish ha'i wattsida deha:donapkya, da:s le'hoł denan otdikya! Hom nana les a:na's kwa's la:ł emma shik'wamme'kya, lesnapde da: la:ł hom denan ukkya. Da:s ałna't ho' a:kya, ko:wi hołk'yan ho' i:de'chunan, chims ho' kokko upkwin de'chikya.

Hish ho' deshlannant ho's yalukwin kwadokya. Ho' a:łashshik, "Ko'n don dewanan a:deyaye?" yanikinan i:mukya. Kwa' dem dena:na:wamme' ho' beykya, yam ho' nana an denan łey' iyan'ona. Doms uhs'ona akkya about it to where I almost lost it again. However, I did not want to go back to the house another time!

Finally, I sang the song for the kiva group, and when I got home, I told my grandfather that I did what he had asked me. He was very pleased and gave me some change to buy some chico sticks. He said that he was feeling fine now. Later that day I heard the dancers singing the new song in the big plaza.

Such is the way I learned. Now let us all learn. Let's learn a dance together.

(When in a Native American community, the "Virginia Reel," and when in a non-Native community, the Sade:chi:we ["Split Circle"] Dance.)

END

hom ayyammo'ayena:wap da:s ełt ho' yam denan okk'yakkya. Ełt le' leyadipde, kwa's la:ł ik'wałt ho' yam k'yakkwin a:na'man' iyahkya!

Chimi so' ki:wihtsi'an upbon' a:wan ho' denan dena:kya, lesnans ho' yam k'yak'wan de'chinan, yam nana adinekkya, hom ko'na' anhe:doshna'kowa ho' lesde lewukya. Hom nana hish ele itse'makukya, akkya ho' chico sticks wo:dihdun'on akkya yam hek'uhmo: wopbona'kowa hom a:wukkya. Lehap hom nana benans, kwa's an ko'hoł ley'amme ke:si le'kwekkya. Uhsi'de yadon delana:'ap dehwit'an luk denan chim'ona odi:kwe' dene:napkya.

Le'n leya' ho' yanikwadikya. Hana't hon demł'ona a:wiyanikwadinna. Hon odin łana' a:wiyanikwadinna.

(Honk'wat A:ho'i'de' a:wan łuwal'an dek'yannuwap, "Virginia Reel" dek'yanna. Da:ch'at hoł kwa' a:ho'i'de a:wan łuwal'an de'ammap, odin łana odi:wa.)

LE:WI

Individual **Contributors**

Anne Beckett, *of Santa Fe, New Mexico, was the executive director of Zuni A:shiwi Publishing from 1995-1998, and first proposed this book, which she has continued to help guide.*

Tommy Bledsoe, *of St. Augustine, Florida, is an artist, administrator, and teacher. A native of Scott County, Virginia, he began working with Appalshop as a June Appal recording artist in 1974 and was an actor and musician in the Roadside Theater ensemble from 1981 to 1996.*

Gregory Cajete, *of Santa Clara Pueblo, New Mexico, is an assistant professor of education at the University of New Mexico and dean of the Center for Research and Cultural Exchange at the Institute of American Indian Arts in Santa Fe. He is the author of* Look to the Mountain *and* Native Science, Natural Laws of Interdependence.

Hal Cannon, *of Salt Lake City, Utah, is the founding director of the Western Folklife Center in Elko, Nevada, and its well known offspring the Cowboy Poetry Gathering. He is a writer, musician, and producer, currently working on a public television documentary,* Why the Cowboy Sings.

Individual contributors, continued

Dudley Cocke, *of Norton, Virginia, is the director of Roadside Theater. He is a stage director, media producer, and author of numerous essays about cultural policy and rural life. His essays have appeared recently in* American Theatre *magazine and the periodicals* Wind *and* Theater.

Kim Neal Cole, *of Castlewood, Virginia, became a member of the Roadside Theater ensemble in 1986 after seeing the theater perform at her high school. She is a performer on stage and screen and is currently working on several community oral history and story collecting projects.*

Angelyn DeBord, *of Nickelsville, Virginia, is a visual artist, playwright, and performer. She often tours her solo performances which are drawn from her Appalachian and Native American heritages. She was a part of the Roadside Theater ensemble from 1975 to 1991.*

Tony Earley, *a native of Rutherfordton, North Carolina, is an assistant professor of English at Vanderbilt University. His fiction and nonfiction writing has appeared in a variety of publications, including the* New Yorker *and* Harper's, *and his recent novel,* Jim the Boy, *is being adapted for television.*

Wilfred Eriacho, Sr., *of Zuni, New Mexico, is the director of bilingual education, administering the Zuni Public School District's operational bilingual education program and the Title VII System Improvement Grant. He devotes much of his time to his kiva.*

Jane Hillhouse, *of Kingsport, Tennessee, is a graphic designer and the owner of Hillhouse Graphic Design, which has won numerous awards including a National Clarion Award for her work as art director of* Storytelling Magazine. *She plays violin in the Kingsport Symphony Orchestra.*

Arden Kucate, *of Zuni, New Mexico, is a founding member of Idiwanan An Chawe. Presently, he is an elected member of the Zuni Tribal Council and holds a high position in his medicine society.*

Dinanda Laconsello, *of Zuni, New Mexico, is a performer with Idiwanan An Chawe and works as a teacher's aid in the Zuni Middle School while pursuing a degree in education.*

Liz McGeachy, *of Norris, Tennessee, is a free-lance writer, editor, and musician. She has worked with Roadside Theater on several projects.*

Individual contributors, continued

Paul Neha, *of Zuni, New Mexico, now deceased, was employed by Pueblo Zuni as a carpentry teacher and served on many tribal committees. He held high positions in his religious medicine society and kiva, was a cultural mentor, and proudly served in the United States Marine Corps.*

Donna Porterfield, *of Norton, Virginia, is Roadside Theater's managing director and one of its writers. She coordinated the 1990-1996 Zuni–Roadside artistic exchange and collaboration. Her recent play,* Voices from the Battlefront, *a collaboration with an Appalachian women's shelter, addresses domestic violence.*

Ron Short, *of Big Stone Gap, Virginia, is a member of the Roadside Theater ensemble. He is a composer, performer, and playwright. A collection of his new songs is on the compact disc* Wings to Fly (Copper Creek), *and he is presently writing a new musical,* Two Sweethearts.

Taki Telonidis, *of Salt Lake City, Utah, is senior producer for Western Folklife Center Media where he produces features for public radio and television. He formerly worked for National Public Radio as an award-winning senior producer of* Weekend All Things Considered *and a producer for* Morning Edition.

Edward Wemytewa, *of Zuni, New Mexico, is the founding director of Idiwanan An Chawe. He is a playwright, performer, and visual artist whose prize-winning paintings and sculpture have been exhibited in museums in Arizona and New Mexico. In addition, he works on Zuni language projects through the Zuni Fish and Wildlife Department.*

Dinah Zeiger, *of Denver, Colorado, is an arts consultant and adjunct faculty member at Metropolitan State College of Denver and the University of Colorado-Denver. As a journalist and editor for twenty-five years, she was on the staffs of* The Denver Post, The Wall Street Journal-Europe, Investor's Business Daily, *and McGraw-Hill, Inc.*

Organizational Contributors

Appalshop, *of Whitesburg, Kentucky, is a multi-disciplinary arts and education center telling the Appalachian story from the inside-out in films, theater, music and spoken-word recordings, radio, and books. Appalshop's regional and national residencies support communities' efforts to celebrate their cultural strengths and solve their problems by publicly telling their stories.*

The Western Folklife Center, *of Elko, Nevada, is dedicated to the art of ordinary people in the West. Best known for its Cowboy Poetry Gathering in Elko, the center also produces regular features about the region and its traditions for public radio and television.*

Zuni Rainbow Project, *of Zuni, New Mexico, is the only program sponsored by the Pueblo of Zuni Tribal Administration dealing with preservation and perpetuation of the Zuni language and culture. It supported the founding of Idiwanan An Chawe and has conducted outreach projects with public schools, universities, theaters, and indigenous language organizations.*

Zuni A:shiwi Publishing, *of Zuni, New Mexico, was created in 1995 by members of the Zuni Pueblo. It is the only independent, not-for-profit publisher located on a Native American reservation, and the only one devoted exclusively to preserving and promoting indigenous American cultures through books conceived and written by Native peoples.*

Audio on Compact Disc

Compact Disc

The *Journeys Home* CD has nineteen tracks to make it easy for you to manipulate the recorded material to suit your purposes. For example, a teacher might assemble track 4 (*Hairy Woman Story*), track 6 (*Turkey Girl Story*), and track 15 (*When Storytellers Became Beggars*) for a classroom unit on story and storytelling. Please feel free to combine the tracks as your imagination wills.

The ability to listen carefully is becoming a lost talent, perhaps because most of us find it necessary to turn a deaf ear to the constant noise that surrounds us. We've become accustomed to half-listening. By giving more attention to the CD, with a calm spirit and big ears, we hope that you will enjoy it more.

Journeys Home

Audio Tracks

1 Dust and Dogs (1:19)

2 Two Cultures (2:58)

3 Kumanchi Marching Song/Wings to Fly Song (1:26)

4 Hairy Woman Story (4:35)

5 Harvest Dance [Kumanchi Song] (1:30)

6 Turkey Girl Story (6:36)

7 Zuni and Appalachian Memories (1:50)

8 I Grew Up on a Farm (1:49)

9 Harvest Dance [Kumanchi Marching Song] (1:13)

10 Drop Four Grains (1:09)

11 Zuni Corn Grinding (0:46)

12 Corn Grinding Song (1:51)

13 Keeping the Songs (0:42)

14 Dancing Alone (1:28)

15 When Storytellers Became Beggars (1:24)

16 Zuni Winter [Zuni] (1:53)

17 Zuni Winter [English] (1:16)

18 Bright Morning Star Song (0:36)

19 Kumanchi Marching Song/Wings to Fly Song (1:48)

Storytellers

Kim Neal Cole
Arden Kucate
Dinanda Laconsello
Ron Short
Edward Wemytewa

Singers/Musicians

Appalachia

Ron Short
Kim Neal Cole
Tommy Bledsoe ("Bright Morning Star")
Hal Cannon ("Margaret's Waltz")

Zuni

Bradley Edaakie
Chris Edaakie
Rayland Edaakie
Roger Leekya
Rita Edaakie ("Lullaby")

Production

Executive producer, Dudley Cocke
Recorded and produced by Taki Telonidis with Hal Cannon
With additional direction from Ron Short, Donna Porterfield, and Edward Wemytewa
Recorded Pueblo Zuni, February 8-13, 2000
Additional recording by David Castle, Maggard Sound
Mastered by Alan Maggard at Maggard Sound, Big Stone Gap, Virginia